The Tide

The author

Mark Tuohy has been involved in community development and social work in London for a number of years. He is an established radio dramatist and is currently working on his second novel.

THE TIDE
mark tuohy

Crescent

First published in 2005 by Crescent Books,
an imprint of Mercat Press Ltd
10 Coates Crescent, Edinburgh EH3 7AL
www.crescentfiction.com

ISBN 184183 081X

The publisher acknowledges subsidy from the Scottish Arts Council
towards the publication of this volume.

Set in Myriad Roman at Mercat Press
Printed and bound in Great Britain by
Antony Rowe Ltd

For Kate

one

I think I walked through a park or some open bit where there were mothers with pushchairs and little kids walking and big kids smoking on a bench in the corner and then there were just lots of roads and cars and traffic lights and new housing estates with tidy little gardens and a roundabout with rubbish dumped in the middle and then I don't know what else but then there was this big metal bridge that I remembered from some time before and I walked slowly towards it staring up at the cables and the steel girders and I remember thinking that this was probably what the Golden Gate Bridge would look like if it was a lot smaller and I walked on until I reached the middle of the bridge and then I stopped and leant over the edge looking down at the river staring right into it like you can when you're really thinking and the water looked clear and pure and not filthy like everyone says it is and I could smell the clean air that rose up from its flow and I imagined what it would be like to be a river to just be water forever and I closed my eyes.

I closed my eyes and for a moment I could see the stupid headlines in local newspapers that had never heard of me and I could hear them talking in pubs and trying to work out why but then it all just faded away not mattering anymore and this was about me and no one else and I lifted one foot slowly and wondered if I'd feel close to god or any religious anything with a vision or something but still I knew that wasn't true and I never believed any of it in the first place but when everything comes rushing you have to have something to hang it on and I suppose some kind of god is good enough if you can find one and so I jumped and for a moment everything stood still and everything made sense and I hit the water like I thought I always wanted to but it was cold like I'd never thought of and it pulled me down and for a moment I couldn't breathe and my clothes were strangling me and the tide washed over me like it couldn't care and I didn't care but still suddenly I felt scared and there was no one there and maybe that's how it's meant to be but I could remember things that I'd never seen and my mother was standing over me with a man and a jukebox was playing some stupid song that I would never choose and then suddenly everything went still and I drank in water and the tide lifted me and I was far away sailing into oceans that I had never dreamt of and still I was right on course and at last I was going somewhere but still the water was cold and I was drowning slowly just like I thought I always wanted to.

two

Above the Chinese takeaway at the far end of the high street where the real shops aren't really there anymore only their windows covered with posters for gigs that are already out of date and minicab men hanging around outside half boarded-up offices waiting for the phone to ring. That's where I lived with Margaret. I slept in the bedroom at the back and my window looked out on a huge grey yard and during the day I'd sit there smoking waiting for the buses to show. Most of the time it was just empty and quiet and still like a graveyard where someone had stolen all the headstones but sometimes a bus would creep out of a corner and it would wait there like it was trying to figure out what it was meant to be doing and then suddenly it would spin into turning circles and skids and tip-overs and whatever else buses are tested for before they go out on the road and then it would disappear.

At night I listened to the rattle of the trains coming from beyond the yard and I breathed in motorway traffic and Chinese food and hoped that Margaret wouldn't need changing again. Margaret was my grandmother is my grandmother you can't change things like that and she always told me to call her Margaret and she said if you're given a name then people should use it and so I did. She slept in the front room well lived in it really she never went anywhere else. Everything she needed was in that room the TV the settee the commode the bowl to wash in and her old radio. And then there was me on call across the hall. I didn't mind at first I probably never really minded but it got tiring at the end and it got desperate and it didn't matter what I did but she started to smell of piss all the time and she couldn't even remember my name.

I moved in with Margaret six years ago a few weeks before my thirteenth birthday and she was alright back then. My mum had thrown me out and then run off to Dublin with her latest boyfriend a middle-aged rock singer who had a stupid name like Spez or something who was going to get a new band together and it was going to be called Oscar and he had long grey hair and tattoos on both his buttocks which is something you don't want to know about someone. My mum thought he was funny and she'd never looked after me much anyway and so what was the difference I'd always spent more time at Margaret's than anywhere else and I used to love it when she had her house far away in Connemara near a place with a name I could never say or ever learn to spell. I remembered it was a bed and breakfast and she used to run it with her sister because my grandad had died a long time ago but then when her sister died as well and she got too old she moved over to England to be near my mum and me and I remember being really sad about that and I was still only little but I could see that she was never going to be happy again. All she ever talked about was my grandad who'd died even before I was born and the house that she'd loved and now they were both gone forever. She'd tell me all about the house how it stood on the top of the hill and it had six windows at the front and it was made of old grey stone but half of it was covered in what looked like ivy but was called something else and it would turn to red in October but not for long and you had to watch out for it or you'd miss it and then you'd have to wait for another year. And she talked about the house like it was more important than anything in the world and I got to know it better than I ever did when I used to go there those times when I was young and it started to feel like it was my house as well and Margaret said I would have loved to live there and I knew I would have but she would never say how to get there just that it was in Connemara like in a dream forever. She should have died in that house not in some shitty flat in London smelling of piss. Sometimes I'd get angry when I thought about it too much so I tried not to but I tried not to do a lot of things and you can't control everything sometimes stuff just gets out and that's it you have to deal with it.

That morning when I walked nervously into her room like I knew I was going to find something bad I couldn't see much because the big brown curtains were still closed and so I opened them just slightly and then I saw her in the chair dribbling like she was trying to say something. I went over to her and knelt down and held her cold veiny hand and tried hard to hear the whispered-out words that fell with the saliva down onto her chin and I think she said she loved me and I told her I loved her too very much. And she said I wasn't like my mother and I said thank you and she said I was like the son she never had and then she just said nothing and I started to cry.

It felt like I'd always been crying and when the ambulance woman spoke to me she asked if I was going to be alright and was there anyone else I could call. I said there wasn't there never had been and I'd be okay I just needed time to think. I didn't go to the hospital or the morgue or wherever they take dead people when

they're dead before they get burnt or buried I didn't want to iden-
tify the body I didn't care if it was routine and I didn't care if they
were sorry because Margaret was still with me somewhere and I
wasn't going to let someone tell me she wasn't. The doctor called
round the next day and asked me how I was which was a stupid
question anyway and so I said I was fine and he said they'd managed to contact my mother and I said I didn't want to know and he
was surprised but still he said that sadly she wouldn't be attending
the funeral and I said before he could ask it that anyway no I wasn't
going to the funeral because there was no point. He didn't understand that he thought somebody should go and I said he could go
if he wanted to and he didn't know what to say then and so he just
said he was sorry and walked away. Why do people always say
they're sorry and then walk away when they'd be better off saying
nothing.

I don't know how I ended up at the bridge. I can remember a
bus and a fat man who sat too close to me and he smelt of an
aftershave that could probably be used in chemical warfare but I
didn't say anything and when it stopped I just got off wherever
the bus was and walked. I walked past a building site somewhere
and some workman said he'd like to give me one and I said one
what you wanker because I had long hair and I think I got quite
aggressive and he said sorry mate and laughed which pissed me
off even more so I left it at that. And I knew I was lost but I didn't
care and I wasn't even scared which was odd because I never used
to like going out. Since I'd left school I only really went to the supermarket and the job centre. I didn't want a job but they'd still
put me in job clubs and make me apply for things that I was never
going to do and sign up for stupid courses at places where I would
never go. Sometimes they tried to stop my benefit because I wasn't
trying hard enough or something but the Doctor always came out

with some good excuses for me I think because he knew I was looking after Margaret. That's why I had to do the shopping. I didn't like
the supermarket I didn't like the people in it or that funny bread
smell they spray all over the place but you have to eat and it's the
cheapest place and so it's like they say beggars can't be choosers
and anyway we're all losers in the end. Margaret added the last bit.

three

They led me in pale and shaking. Something had happened back at the main hospital that I didn't understand but I knew I wasn't going home and that this was somewhere else where they were going to care for me and make me well again that's what the social worker said anyway and she seemed nice enough and so I thought she was probably telling the truth. Later on when I remembered what she'd said I got very angry and I would have hit her if I'd seen her until I realised that she meant what she said and she really wanted it to be true but that isn't always enough is it.

They sat me down on a settee that caved in as soon as your bum hit the cushions and I could feel myself sinking down into it and I wondered why the river had taken me here and I wondered that if I sunk far enough down into the settee would it take me somewhere else again but would it be any better. There were too many thoughts and questions and I think I know the answers to be able to concentrate on what this nurse was trying to say to me so I just smiled at her and she smiled back but she looked surprised and a little embarrassed. She was probably about the same age as me. She wrote something down and then she looked back at me and I was listening this time when she said did I want the TV on and I said why not and she turned it on for me and said she'd be back later and so I just watched TV with this woman alone in the corner who kept staring over at me and chewing her lip.

Her name was Anna and she didn't care whether I was well or not or what I was and she was the first person to speak to me without hidden meaning behind her words and so I listened to what she said because she was listening to me and I never told her that she shouldn't chew her lip so much.

It was the next day after breakfast when she came over to the settee and sat down beside me and I was going to move away but she spoke first.

'Do you smoke?'

'Yeah,' I said and she passed me a roll-up she'd already rolled.

'Thanks,' I said and put the cigarette to my lips.

Anna lit my cigarette first and then her own and we both puffed out smoke and I tried not to get the cigarette paper stuck to my lips like I always do unless it's the brown liquorice papers because they're a bit thicker and shiny and they just slip off your lips but anyway it was nice to have a cigarette after breakfast and then Anna said something else.

'Have you been in here before?'

'No.'

'That's probably why I don't recognise you then.'

'Oh.'

Anna took another drag of her cigarette and so I did the same thing.

'It's not a bad place,' Anna said as she let the smoke roll out of her mouth.

'Good,' I said because I didn't know so I might as well take her word for it.

She didn't say anything else after that and so we just smoked and then put our cigarettes out and then she nodded at me and smiled as she got up and wandered off and I smiled at her back and it felt nice.

Later in the morning I had to see the psychiatrist and she didn't say anything I could understand. I had to sit down again which is what everybody does all the time in these places it's like there's no time to do anything because it's all taken up by the sitting down but still they all keep on doing it even the people who should know better like Jane you don't have to call me doctor the psychiatrist. Why did she do all those exams to be a doctor and then not want people to call her doctor. I thought maybe she was in the wrong job only she couldn't come right out and say it not after all those years spent training and her mum and dad being so proud of her and so I suppose you don't have to call me doctor was Jane's way of dealing with it. Anyway Jane I said after she'd finished talking about what section of the mental health act I was under or something and I'd thought about the water again but then got back on the subject anyway Jane I said now I'll tell you all about my life.

I didn't tell her everything because that would have been boring so I just told her the best bits. I told her about how when I was little I used to stay up late dancing to the Clash with my mum in the front room because she didn't have a boyfriend and we'd be getting on really well and the next day I'd be too tired to go to school but she'd write me a note saying I had a cold when I didn't and when I went back to school they'd say I looked very tired and did I really have a cold or was it something else and I'd say I didn't know but my mum said I had a cold so that must be it and anyway did they like White Man in the Hammersmith Palais and they'd say they didn't know it and so I'd sing them the bit about pop reggae and Delroy Wilson the cute operator but still they wouldn't get it and so I'd go right to the end of the song and if Adolf Hitler flew in today they'd send a limousine anyway and I'm the white man in the Palais just looking for fun and still they wouldn't recognise it only giving themselves odd looks and saying but it sounded interesting and so I'd ask them did they know how to roll a cigarette because I did and I knew I wasn't meant to say that and I'd stare straight back at their faces and they wouldn't be sure and then suddenly they'd be really nice to me like I needed their help and when I fell asleep in the class they just took me to the sick room and let me lie down when all the other kids would have to do maths or something. When I talked like this Jane just nodded like she understood like it meant something to her and she kept writing things down but I knew she'd never understand because she didn't want to be called doctor and if she didn't even know what she was then she'd never understand me.

Talking to Jane was like being seven years old and at school again and she would have sent someone round to talk to my mum just like they did but mum wasn't there anymore and Margaret was dead. She asked me who Margaret was but I wouldn't tell her because I didn't want Margaret getting in trouble and because I knew it wasn't her fault.

And then I went quiet because I'd run out of breath and all I really wanted was one of Anna's cigarettes but I didn't want to say anything because I didn't want to upset Jane because I could tell that she was doing her best but that it was never going to be good enough and I felt a bit sorry for her when I thought about it like that. And then she asked me a stupid question like everyone always does when they run out of ideas.

'What do you want most from life?' She asked it like it was the biggest and bravest question in the world.

'Freedom,' I said because that's what Margaret always said was the most important thing of all and you shouldn't let anything else get in the way but still it's the hardest thing to find.

Jane thought a lot about my answer before she said anything and I thought that maybe I was going to get away for that cigarette after all but then she came out with the usual.

'And what exactly do you mean by freedom?'

For fuck's sake I was trying to help her out I was going along with it just how she wanted but now she was really getting on my nerves and so I stood up and told her I was going out to have a cigarette and I wasn't coming back until she sorted out who she was and could come up with some half-decent questions. She smiled when I said that like she knew something I didn't so I had to say something else because I couldn't leave it at that.

'Why don't you just piss off,' I said not too loud but like I really meant it and I did and I went straight out of the door slamming it back as I went.

four

I didn't talk to anyone else after all that don't call me doctor Jane bollocks and when it got to night and I got into bed I closed my eyes and I could still hear some people making stupid noises like they were trying to sound mental on purpose or something but soon I forgot all about that and I was in bed upstairs in the attic of Margaret's bed and breakfast house looking up through the slanty window at the stars and the moon that I could see from the glow that it was hiding behind a cloud but I didn't mind because the glow was soft and gentle and you can imagine a lot more about the moon when it doesn't make it obvious and I thought that the moon was a friend that was waiting for me and wondered if I was going to come out and play but of course I wouldn't because it was really late but it was nice of the moon to think that anyway. Earlier on my mum had come back from the pub with some man who had a cigarette in his mouth and couldn't say his words properly and I'd thought that maybe there was something wrong with him so I'd try to be nice but then he fell over and mum laughed and Margaret said that she shouldn't be bringing drunken strangers back to the house and I thought that was funny because it was usually mum that did all the falling over but I just kept quiet and looked at all of them. Mum asked me what my problem was and I didn't know what to say because I didn't think I had a problem and then she said we were meant to be on bloody holiday and that I should try cheering up for a change and that was when Margaret told her to shut up and that enough was enough whatever that means and they started shouting at each other and the man fell asleep and his cigarette fell out of his mouth and onto his tummy and I could see it starting to burn a hole in the bottom of his jumper and I tried to tell mum and she told me to shut up because it was always me that caused everything and Margaret wasn't having any of that or something and the man woke up when the cigarette started to burn a hole in his tummy and he said fuck it and I'm going home and mum said and I'm going with you and Margaret said and don't bloody come back and she didn't. But I was happy to be looking at the sky because it's so far away from fuck this and fuck that because it's just a high and peaceful place where if you screamed and shouted it wouldn't matter because everything is so big your sound would disappear and so you couldn't shout even if you wanted to and so even if you could get there which you never could it's the best place. Not being somewhere is always the best place to be and the sky is the greatest big nowhere and it's always there and it covers everything and as I looked up through the slanty window I could see the clouds moving slowly like maybe they'd found somewhere to go and for a moment I was worried that they were going to leave the moon behind but then I could see more stars appearing and they did their twinkle twinkle as the moon came out from behind its cloud and then I closed my eyes and I didn't need to dream.

And when I woke up the mental people were fast asleep and there were no more looney noises and so I suppose the drugs had started to work and so maybe everyone would soon be well again. Maybe everyone would sit down for breakfast and talk about how things were going to be and everyone would be so clear about everything that they wouldn't need the cigarettes anymore and they would go out and get on buses and trains and wear suits and shirts and nice long dresses and show everyone else how good it is to be alive and smile with clean teeth and get serious when you're meant to and know about what's going on in the world but not be scared of it. It was good to think good things Margaret had always said that she said how can you do good things if you don't think good things first and of course she was right but sometimes the thinking's the hardest part.

That morning I was sitting next to Anna at breakfast and I started to tell her all about it and I was quite excited because it was like I was starting to work things out but Anna just quickly looked sideways at me and said the problem was too much thinking and not enough listening and then she looked back down at the piece of toast on her plate and picked it up and took another bite like there was nothing left to be said. And at first I was quiet wondering about what she had said but then I thought that Anna must have been talking about the wrong kind of thinking the kind you get stuck in and can't get out of and Margaret never got stuck and I tried to explain that to Anna but I don't think she could hear me because it didn't matter what I said it didn't seem to make any difference. Then when she had finished her toast and drunk down the last gulp of her tea she looked at me again and said, 'It's good to think good things only if you can.' I still wasn't sure what she meant so I asked.

'How do you know if you don't try?'

'Everybody tries, but not forever. Sometimes you just stop, sometimes you know that the good things will always be too far away to see. Sometimes you just get tired trying. You can't change the world.'

'You can still look out for the good bits.'

'Only if you know where to start.' She said it like I shouldn't ask anymore and so I didn't.

five

Another week later and the stale smoke from the smoking room was nearly turning me away from cigarettes so I decided to go outside and sit on the bench. I sat down and looked at the wet grass with bits of autumn leaves mushed into it and the wind was blowing a soft cloud of rain across my face which was nice but it made it hard to light a cigarette so I cupped my hands around the match flame and dropped my head in under the wind and the tobacco started to burn. It felt nice out there in the fresh air with the smoke warming my lungs and the smell of the match and the cigarette was like when I first started to smoke in the park and we used to set fire to the dustbins when everyone was walking around saying how lovely it was how the autumn leaves were so many browns and reds and oranges and then they'd say oh god the dustbin's on fire and where's the park keeper and we'd laugh and of course he was nowhere to be seen and even if there ever was a park keeper what could he do anyway.

I lost myself in thoughts of great days when nothing mattered and you could do anything you wanted because we never got caught and we could have ruled the world if we wanted to and I could remember the faces but I'd forgotten the names but I remembered what we did to the school library and how we poured vim bloody all over the place and still we were only ten and kiss chase was just a laugh and there was the day when we curled back the wires and crawled under the fence into the overgrown garden next to the school playground where there was the old empty house that was all boarded up and there was a big falling-down shed as well where we went in and scrunched up all the bits of newspaper and lit them with matches and when the fire started to burn we ran away and crawled back under the fence into the playground hoping that the dinner ladies especially the one with the long nose and too small eyes wouldn't see us and they didn't. We waited and watched until just above the bushes in the overgrown garden we could see small clouds of smoke starting to float up towards the hot summer sun and we didn't say anything and we laughed when the smoke got bigger and started to blow everywhere and some little kid ran up to the dinner lady with the too small eyes and was telling her all about a fire in the woods and she was telling him to stop being silly until she turned round and could see all the smoke and now even a flame and then she ran off to call the fire brigade. And when they came we watched the fire engines and the water firing out everywhere and the teacher let us watch instead of doing our lesson saying how dangerous fire was and we should all be very careful and I remember my friend was next to me and we both grinned a secret grin knowing they would never catch us because we were like Butch Cassidy and The Sundance Kid only better and then I looked up and out at the hospital walls that were around the square where I was sitting trying to smoke in the misty rain and I thought maybe you do get caught in the end and maybe that's why I was here and I didn't like to think like that because that's when the clouds come down and crush you and you can't get up and you can't breathe and I was glad when Anna came out and sat down next to me.

'How's it going?' She said with her long brown hair being blown wet by the wind.

'Not too bad.' I tried to smile but I don't think she believed me.

'Is the medication working?' She sounded like she was probably joking making herself sound like a nurse or a doctor or something but I couldn't really tell so I answered her like it was a real question.

'I think so, I feel a lot calmer now.'

Anna smiled.

'You'll be going home soon then.'

I didn't know what to say because I hadn't thought about going home because there wasn't any home to go to and you don't have to call me doctor Jane didn't talk about things like that it was somebody else's job and they were going to talk to me about it when I was ready but I don't think they had and so probably I wasn't ready.

'I don't know,' I said.

Anna looked sadly back at me and I caught her eyes for a moment but then I looked away and puffed hard on my cigarette before it went out on its own. Anna had nice eyes they were brown and a little sad and tired but there was still a sparkle in there and she was probably about forty or something or maybe older or younger it was hard to tell but I liked her and she liked me but I didn't know why.

'Maybe you should ask them when you're going home,' she said. 'They usually tell you when you ask.'

'I'll ask them,' I said but I didn't know who to ask.

'Why don't you ask Paula?'

'Yeah, I will,' I said.

Anna smiled again and I thought about how she didn't say much but she always said the right things and I was glad that she did and I would speak to Paula because she was the young one I'd seen on my first day and she understood about the Clash and she thought it was good me dancing with my mum and she didn't talk too much either and I don't think she liked you don't have to call me doctor Jane because of the way she looked when Jane would come into the room and tell her to do things that she would have done anyway and she didn't need to be told.

I looked back at Anna and she'd looked away and she was chewing her lip again just like she always does when there's nothing left to say and I looked at her hair and it was getting wet and the rain was getting heavier and I said maybe we should go back inside now and she said for me to go and that she'd be there in a minute. I got up and walked slowly back towards the ward and just before I opened the door and went back inside I looked back at Anna and she was looking over the rooftops up at the sky and into the rain and I hoped that she was thinking good things and that it wasn't all sadness.

I thought a lot about Anna and the words she said because there was a lot of time to think as the days went slowly by which was okay because I needed the time to work out what it was about the river and the jumping in and why that still didn't scare me. Anna said why should it you were cleansing yourself to start again she said I didn't realise it at the time but I needed to be reborn and something deep in my subconscious knew that and that's what took me to the bridge but not for an ending like everyone thought but for a new beginning. I said I could have died and Anna said I wasn't meant to but just in case I shouldn't try it again and she had laughed which was good because she didn't laugh enough.

I surrounded myself with all those thoughts of Anna as I walked back inside and over to the plastic seats where I sat down near the TV where no one was watching whatever it was that was on. And I thought about what it was like living on a psychiatric ward and it was alright really even them giving me all those drugs that in the end I just took to be polite but the thing was I didn't really talk to anyone except Anna. I'd say hello to other people and maybe even smile or say something about what the weather was like outside but I didn't properly talk to anyone else although sometimes when I played table tennis with Satvinder he would talk. He would talk a lot but it was always him explaining to me that no one's mad really it's just something that's been constructed to make money for the drugs companies and the psychiatrists who invented madness in the first place. The thing was Satvinder would always beat me at table tennis even when he wouldn't stop talking and at the end he would say, 'So there you are, the mad man was made up, he was made up to keep people in their place, to moderate their behaviour. It is not said but everyone knows if you are too different you will not be tolerated, you will be sectioned under the mental health act and taken away. It is a kind political persecution only worse, you are not persecuted for what you believe you are persecuted for who you are.' And he would nod in a way that was almost a bow and hold his hands together like he was ready to pray and then make the sign by moving his hands up and down and I would do the same and nod back to him as well and I liked that for a moment it felt like it was us against the world and no one else could ever understand maybe even not Anna and so I always looked forward to the next time we could play table tennis. But that was the only time we talked and maybe we should have tried harder but maybe not because it was good as it was and anyway I had Anna to talk to about all the other things and I hoped that Satvinder had someone else to talk to as well.

o o o

I didn't see the nurse called Paula for a few days but when I did she said that it was all sorted and that there was a vacancy at the hostel and did I want to go and have a look that afternoon and that someone from the community team would show me round and they'd be the one who'd be looking after me and wasn't that great.

'What hostel?' I said. 'You never said anything about a hostel.' Paula looked a bit disappointed when I said that but I had to say something because she wasn't making any sense.

'Don't you remember that meeting we had with Jane and the others? That case conference where we made that plan so that you'd have somewhere to go and someone to look after you.'

'I don't need anyone to look after me I just need somewhere to live. Why can't I go back to the flat?'

'Because you're not ready.'

'Not ready for what?'

'Not ready to be on your own.'

'I've always been on my own.'

'This is different. I'm sorry, I thought you'd remember.'

I did, vaguely.

'What's the hostel like then?'

'It's a big old house…'

'And it's falling down like they always are.'

'Not at all, they've just redone the whole place. It's really nice, honestly. Why don't you have a look for yourself? With the CPN.'

'The what?'

Paula went on to tell me what a great thing a Community Psychiatric Nurse was and how they supported you in the community and loads of other community stuff and I think she really liked the word community so I just let her say it again and again because I liked the sound of her voice and the way she always put her hand gently on my shoulder when she thought she was telling me big things.

And so in the afternoon I went to look at the place with a CPN person called Dougie who had a dodgy-looking goatee beard but he was alright really and his car was full of sweet wrappers and yesterday's papers and all that and when he put a tape on it was U2 and he said did I like U2 and so I said yes because it was the polite thing to do but it was hard to have a conversation with Bono going on like he does and so when we parked up outside this big house and Dougie smiled and said as long as that's alright with you I just said yeah fine which must have been the right answer because Dougie looked quite pleased with himself when he got out of the car and you could tell he thought he'd done a good job which maybe he had.

Dougie rang the bell and I stood and waited behind him. It was a long time before anybody answered and Dougie was about to push the bell again when the door was slowly opened by a woman wearing yellow rubber gloves who didn't look very pleased to see us but Dougie smiled at her anyway like he probably smiles at everyone because of him always wanting things to be alright with everybody. 'Alright there Vicky,' he said just like you would have expected him to.

'Not bad,' she said but didn't even bother to try and look like she meant it.

'Is Sally in?'

'She's gone to the shops.'

'Do you know when she'll be back?'

'Ages probably, she only just went.'

'Is anybody else around?'

'No. Good job too, it gives me a chance to get the place cleaned up. Do you want to come in and wait or what?'

'I just wanted to let Michael here have a quick look round, if that's okay with you.'

'It's not up to me. If you want to come in then come in.'

'Thanks,' he said and showed me in as Vicky sort of smiled at me like I was a sick dog and it wasn't really my fault so she should at least try to be nice.

Vicky shut the door behind us and then disappeared to do whatever cleaning it was she was doing and me and Dougie stood alone in the big hall of the big empty house that smelt of new paint and stale cigarettes.

'Let's start downstairs then,' said Dougie cheerfully and I don't think he'd noticed that Vicky obviously thought he was a bit of a prick and probably a lot of people thought that because everyone doesn't always want everything to be alright like he does they just want things to be okay and still have lots of stuff to moan about.

We walked along the hall towards the back of the house and went through a heavy door that shut itself slowly with one of those metal arms and then we were in the biggest kitchen I'd ever been in. There was a great big long table in the middle and windows and a door at the side that looked into a garden that looked like it needed a gardener but the sun was coming in and it shone on a huge great silver toaster like the ones they have in cafes that can do loads of bits of bread at once and everything was clean and new like no one had ever come into the room and there were no dirty plates or tea bag stains by the bin and I tried to work out where they kept all the food but I couldn't.

'It's nice isn't it,' said Dougie.

'It's big.'

'Very.' And Dougie started to walk around the kitchen and over to the windows to look out.'Shame about the garden though.'

I thought the garden was alright even if it did need a gardener because I'd never lived in a house with a garden and you could tell probably Dougie had but I didn't say anything and Dougie started to hum a tune as he looked out and it had to be U2 didn't it and I even recognised the song from something they played a lot on the radio just after Margaret died. It was the one that went on about being stuck in a moment and you can't get out of it and I used to listen closely to the words even if it was Bono singing because in a way some of it made sense to me then and later like when he said *the water is warm till you discover how deep* I wondered did he really know like I did or was he just trying to be clever and at the end it says *It's just a moment this time will pass* but without saying how and did that mean that if you just waited long enough things would be okay and I could never work it out and if I was ever to meet Bono I would ask him and anyway I'd like to see what he was really like because maybe he's not as bad as he sounds like Dougie humming the tune badly when it's actually a good song.

Dougie stopped humming and came back from the world of U2.'Shall we have a wander then?' Said like one of those questions that isn't and he started to head for the door with the metal arm and I waited for him to open it and show me out because I could see that was how he wanted to do things.

We went into the TV room which looked like a TV room with new furniture and a nice big telly with probably a video or DVD player or something underneath and the only thing that looked old was a line of worn-out paperback books on one of the shiny white shelves. The books looked sad like they didn't want to be there anymore but someone had told them they had to stay even though they would still probably always be ignored forever and that was how it was and there was nothing you or me or anyone else could do about it.

'I wouldn't mind moving in myself,' said Dougie while I was still feeling sorry for the books. 'Someone's spent a lot of trouble giving this place the right kind of feel. You know, more like a home than a hostel.'

'A mental home?' I couldn't help myself it was the obvious thing to say.

'No, I don't mean it like that, I mean, you know, a home where people live. A normal house.'

'For normal people.' I was taking the piss but Dougie missed it.

'Yeah.' Dougie looked like he was thinking and I waited. 'We're all normal people.' And that was it he'd made his point and I nodded and we moved out of the TV room to look at the hall and then up the stairs to look at a bathroom that Vicky was still cleaning and then a lot of closed doors because everyone was out and so no one could show us their bedroom which Dougie said was a shame but I wasn't bothered because why would I want to look into someone else's bedroom full of all their things.

We got back into the car after Dougie had called up goodbye to Vicky from the front door and she hadn't answered but he said she probably didn't hear but I thought she couldn't be bothered with some CPN who wants everything to be alright when she's got toilets to clean. So Dougie drove off and he didn't put a tape on which was good but instead he had his things to say.

'So do you think you'd be alright there?'

'Looks okay.'

'It's got to be better than staying on the ward.'

'I don't mind the ward.'

'But you're ready to move on.'

'I suppose so.'

'You'll be fine, really. And it's not like you're suddenly going to be on your own or anything. There's the woman Sally who runs the place, she's great, you can always talk to her. And there's the people you'll be living with and if all else fails, me.' The last bit was meant to be a joke and so I laughed a little but Dougie was the kind of person who shouldn't be allowed to make jokes if that was the kind of stuff he was going to come up with. 'Seriously though,' he went on trying to sound serious, 'I'll always be there on the end of the phone as well as calling round to see how you're getting on. When we get back to the hospital I'll give you my mobile number. Even if I'm not about it diverts to somebody else who'll be able to speak to you.'

'When do I move in?'

'So it's alright with you, you understand the deal?'

'I think so.'

'Great. I'll have a word with Jane to see where we're at and then I can get back to you with a date.'

I laughed. Dougie smiled.

'What's so funny?'

'Doesn't anyone ever call her doctor?'

'I don't know, never thought about it really. I don't think so. Why?' I smiled.

'Just wondered.'

And the car drove on and I wasn't happy and I wasn't sad and Dougie was doing his best for me and I didn't even mind the traffic that we got stuck in I just wanted this time to pass and get on with the next bit.

After Dougie had finished his whatever he had to say with you don't have to call me doctor Jane he came out of her room smiling and said 'It's your turn now,' like we were both in it together and it was us against the head teacher or the social worker or the woman in the job centre who would always smile without meaning it and so I nodded back at Dougie and went in and sat down in the seat that sunk down forever and waited for what Jane would say.

'Well?' she said.

'What?' I said.

'Do you feel ready?'

I laughed, the way she said it all serious, I couldn't help myself.

'Go ahead, make my day,' I said still grinning.

'What?' She said.

'You just sounded like a film, that's all.'

'Oh,' she said and I could tell that she was thinking because she touched her earring like she always does when she's about to say something big and stupid. 'Do you see your life as a film Michael?'

'Only sometimes.'

'When, for instance?' She sounded interested now.

'When someone says something that's a line from a film.'

'And you think that's what I did?'

'It is what you did.'

'I don't think so, or at least perhaps more significantly, I'm certainly not aware of it even if I did.'

She was being stupid on purpose so I explained it to her very slowly like when she told me all about the Mental Health Act.

'You said do you feel ready, like Clint Eastwood says do you feel lucky.'

'You thought I was being Clint Eastwood?'

'No, Dirty Harry.'

'I see,' she said but I could see that she didn't. Maybe she'd never seen the film or maybe she was just taking the piss the way doctors do but either way it didn't matter because she wasn't worth the effort.

Jane wrote down some more notes and then she went on about the hostel and how it was a wonderful opportunity and I'd get all the support I needed for as long as I needed but she didn't say how long and they would monitor my progress which I think was meant to make me feel good but again it made me think of school and people watching me waiting for the change that would never happen. Then she started talking about my future and how it would be and maybe starting off with an ordinary job and Sally and Dougie could help and that would be just to get back into the swing of things whatever she meant by that and then it would be who knows what from there and everything would be all up to me and making my way in the world and she made it sound that in the end I could do whatever I wanted like when I was running free and young and in the park but I knew that was bollocks and so did she.

When Jane had finished all that she did her famous last words. 'So,' she said, 'there's nothing to be worried about. You've your whole life ahead of you, we're only here if you need us.'

'Good,' I said without really knowing what it was that was good.

It felt hard explaining it all to Anna when we sat with cups of tea on the big chairs near the TV but both looking out of the window all the time at leaves being blown along the path because they had no choice. It was just hard to say the right things. When I said it was going to be tomorrow she smiled maybe sadly and softly rubbed my back saying everything would be fine and then there was nothing else to say.

six

The hostel wasn't too bad you had your own room with your own TV and there was a kettle and a small sink and downstairs there was a big table where everyone would eat and there'd be one main meal everyday and anything else you had to buy yourself. Then there was Sally who was white but had dreadlocks and she lived in one of the rooms and she was kind of in charge and if you had any problems like Jane and Dougie had said you could go to her and she helped sort out my benefit and bought me a poster of the sea to put on my wall and she was good at cooking vegetable curry but not much else and so me and a couple of the others did most of the cooking.

Apart from Sally there were five people including me. John was old and talked to himself all the time and got in trouble for collecting stuff from rubbish bins and putting it in his wardrobe but he'd always say hello if he saw you. Zoë was very fat and wore black lipstick and talked about star signs all the time and said she would always be twenty-one but must have been at least thirty. Norma never talked to anyone not even herself and she was always disappearing and then coming back again but she walked very slowly so I don't think she ever got far and she looked old enough to die. And then there was Jamie who had every record the Sex Pistols had ever released even the same songs that were just on different record labels and he told me how they did the deal in front of Buckingham Palace and wasn't that great and he had a T-shirt with a picture of a single decker bus on it and where there was the sign to say where it was going it just said Nowhere but I never asked him why because I could tell I was meant to know and he'd wear it nearly all the time and it never got old so I thought he probably had loads of the same T-shirts in his room.

One morning I was sitting at the big table eating four pieces of toast and peanut butter and I was watching John go out the back door with his pockets full of plastic bags when Zoë came into the room and sat down next to me and I was thinking I better eat my toast quickly or she'd want some but she didn't and she just looked at me like I wasn't even eating.

'Do you know what it says for you this week?' She said.

I finished what was in my mouth which was a lot and looked round at her.

'In the stars?'

'Yeah.'

'No.' I had another quick bite.

'It says if you're honest with yourself then you'll discover what it is that you're looking for.'

'Oh.'

'So what are you looking for?'

'I don't know.'

'Then you'll have to try being more honest with yourself.'

'So how do you do that?'

'I don't know. It says you have to find the answers from within.'

'It never makes it easy does it.' I finished up the last piece of toast and thought I'd finished the conversation quite well and that now Zoë would go back to her room and play some loud music like she did most of every day apart from when Sally went in to talk to her but she just sat there and looked like she was thinking.

'I don't think you believe in the stars,' she said.

'I don't believe in anything.'

'You must do.'

'Why?'

'Because if you don't believe in anything then you've got nothing to guide you.'

'I don't need any guiding I know where I'm going.'

'You only think you do and that's the problem.'

'What are you on about?'

'Everybody needs something or someone. Even you Michael.'

She sounded really smug when she said that and suddenly I didn't like the way the conversation was going and I thought Zoë should shut up and stay in her room because I didn't need to hear all this going round the houses stuff that would never make any sense it just got you worried because it made you think that nothing really means anything and that we're all on our own and that everything else is made up to make people feel better when no one wants to know the truth and it's better not to think about all that. And then Zoë said something else and I didn't catch what it was but I knew I wouldn't like it and so I stood up and told her.

'Piss off back to your room and listen to Nirvana, I'm going to work.' As I walked out the door I felt good again and I didn't care what Zoë felt she should shut up more often.

I had to wait ages for the bus but I was early anyway and so I lit a cigarette and tried to listen to the leaves blowing over the pavement and into the road but every time there was a big gust of wind the traffic would get louder and so I didn't hear much but it looked good the way they tumbled and twirled across the road like they didn't care whether they were going to get to the other side or not.

The bus took me to the supermarket where I worked. Sally had helped me fill the form in and told me not to worry about the interview because you don't have to be a brain surgeon to work in a supermarket which the way she said it I think might have upset people who work in supermarkets all their lives but then again maybe they would agree and it's only a job after all and anyway what Sally said must have helped because I got the job. I was happy at first that they didn't put me on the tills because they thought I could do without the stress although I wasn't bothered either way it was good to be doing shelves because there were lots of times when you could sneak off for a cigarette and there was this big fat bloke called Mark and he'd come with me and we'd have a laugh talking about what wankers all the supervisors were even though some of them weren't that bad and you could almost feel sorry for them the way they thought they had an important job to do but all the customers treated them like they were as stupid as the rest of us and the branch manager would say hello to them but only know their names if they were wearing their identity badges.

I spent the day at work doing all the usual stuff only it was mainly a soft drinks and wine day because I remember Vincent my supervisor telling me to hurry up and stock the bloody shelves or there won't be any wine for anyone to buy and the branch manager doesn't like it when people complain saying we've run out of things and so I better get my act together which I did but I still had a quick cigarette with Mark and we both agreed that Vincent was the biggest wanker of the lot but what can you do you've just got to get on with it and so we did and I was glad when my shift was over and I decided to walk all the way home to give me time to get the place out of my head. It was dark and windy and wet like everyone always says autumn is but so what I liked it a lot only I could do without the Christmas that came afterwards but anyway raindrops were blowing across my face and my hair was getting wet and I wondered what Anna was doing and would I ever see her again and I know Margaret would have liked her and it was sad that they would never meet each other but I suppose if Margaret hadn't liked Anna I wouldn't have known what to do so probably things had worked out for the best. It was funny thinking about Anna the way things kept making me think of her and I couldn't help it and so I didn't think about Margaret so much and I thought maybe that meant something but it probably only meant I was thinking about Anna and anyway Margaret would always be there when I needed her.

When I got back to the hostel everyone was sitting round the kitchen table. Sally was making a roll up and nearly everyone else was smoking something as well apart from John who said that cigarettes were sold to kill subversives and that roll ups were just as bad but only worse because of all the time you wasted making them but no one listened to John because he was the man with plastic bags stuffed in all his pockets. I tried just to go upstairs because I didn't want one of those big silent meetings where Sally waited for us all to talk but we never would because we had too much to think about and it was all stuff that was better kept to yourself otherwise things would be written down and Sally would say it was her job to help us and then later the CPN would want to talk it through with you when you'd forgotten what it was you'd said anyway and so it was better to keep quiet and not waste anybody's time. I'd walked past them and got to the bottom of the stairs when Sally called me back.

'Michael, could you just come here a minute? We've got something we need to talk about.'

That was how it always was with we've got something to talk about always meaning she'd got something to talk about and we were all going to have to listen and then try not to think about too many other things so that when she asked us what we thought we didn't just say about what and not have a clue what was going on because that always made her look sad and no one wanted to make Sally sad because she was nice really and always trying to do the best for all of us but I think it was always going to be too much for her in the end. Anyway I walked back into the kitchen.

'Thank you,' she said and she smiled and I sat down where I always sat and I looked out of the window into the garden that was growing everywhere but I always thought it knew where it wanted to go as long as people would leave it alone for long enough. And I kept looking outside as everyone else around the table John and Jamie and Zoë watched Sally's fingers fiddle with her roll up that was never going to be rolled up unless she managed to steady her right hand that I could see in the reflection in the window would probably only calm down when she'd said whatever it was she wanted to say to us.

'Do you want any help with that?' Zoë said and Sally looked embarrassed.

'Yeah, thanks.' Sally passed the roll up across the table to Zoë and I stopped staring out of the window and I looked down at the table and I could see the little specks of tobacco that the paper had left behind and it was like the trail left by a tug boat going along the river and I wondered if anyone else had noticed but they were watching Zoë make the roll up and then hand it back to Sally saying there you are and then Sally smiling like she always does and saying thanks again. She lit her cigarette and then went back to talking to all of us.

'Now that you're all here I just wanted to…'

'Norma's not here.' John interrupted quickly like he always does when he's got something to say but which isn't very often.

'I know John and I'm afraid she won't be and that's what I want to talk about.'

'Is she dead?' I asked which I thought was a fair enough question because she was old and always getting lost but still the others all gave me funny looks apart from Sally.

'No, Norma's not dead.'

'Good,' said John and I looked at him and he looked straight back. 'There's too many dead people in the world,' he said and then looked away again and had a look on his face like he'd given away a secret.

'Norma,' Sally continued, 'has moved on.'

'So she is dead.' Zoë laughed but I could tell from the look on John's face that she shouldn't have said that but Zoë never noticed how things said meant different things to different people and so you should always be careful what you say especially saying someone's dead when they're not.

'Okay, sorry, bad choice of words. I'm just trying to say that Norma has gone to stay somewhere else and she won't be coming back.'

Everyone didn't know what to say all at the same time and Sally looked down at the table.

'Ever?' said John. Sally looked up at him and nodded slowly.

'I'm sorry, I know it would have been better if she could have said goodbye but there's nothing we can do about that now.'

'What happened?' asked Jamie.

'I don't really know, all I know is that earlier today Norma arrived at the hospital in a terrible state and they admitted her straight away.'

'Maybe she'll come back when she's well again,' said John who was already talking far more than he ever did but that wasn't good it was sad.

'I think she's going to be in hospital for quite a while and whenever she does get out she'll need to stay somewhere with more support,' said Sally like she'd read it out of a book and didn't know whether it was true or not.

'Are they going to put her in an old people's home then?' I asked.

'It'll be somewhere where she'll be well cared for.' I knew then from Sally's answer that she didn't know anything about Norma only that she wasn't coming back and I could see that it was all too much for John who got up rustling the plastic bags in his pockets so he didn't have to hear anything else and went into the hall and then we heard the front door bang and John didn't come back for a long time.

Sally then told us that after she'd cleared up Norma's room somebody else called Anna would be moving in next week and I wondered if it could be the same one but didn't think it could be.

seven

I was sitting at the kitchen table on my own trying to work out whether or not I was going to make a bacon sandwich because I could never cook the bacon just how I liked it and because it always made me think about how Margaret always used to cook my bacon just right when she could walk about properly but now that seemed so long ago and it was like there was a huge empty space between me and Margaret and I was never going to be able to get back across to her and that was something that made me feel very alone and so I was glad when Sally walked into the room.

'I'd like to introduce you to our new housemate,' she said which was weird because it was like Big Brother only none of us were ever going to win any money or get jobs on kid's TV but at least there weren't cameras in our bedroom and Davina whatever her name was was never going to sit me down on a sofa and put her arm round me pretending that she liked me with her always acting like she was like the mother or big sister of everyone she probably never wanted to see again.

Sally held open the door and Anna walked in with a smile which was different because she wasn't chewing her lip. I didn't know what to say because Anna suddenly looked beautiful in a way that I didn't think she would and so I smiled back but I was thinking that she was so different and a lot older than me and I'd hoped it would be her but still I couldn't think of the right words and so it was good that Anna spoke first.

'Hello Michael. So we're back together again.'

'Yeah,' I said which I knew wasn't enough but it was the best I could do and Anna just stood there looking happy and not minding what I said and maybe not even hearing because she just went on and said could she make some coffee and I said yeah again and Sally said make yourself at home Anna and Michael will show you where everything is and so I got up and showed her and Sally left the room and me and Anna made coffee together without saying anything because we didn't need to.

At night when I went to bed late after too much TV I went up the stairs quietly and I stopped outside Anna's room because she'd gone to bed early and I listened to see if I could hear her breathing because I wanted to make sure she was okay but I couldn't hear anything and so I sat down and waited and I listened out like I always used to with Margaret in case she wanted me and so I knew this wasn't going to be easy and you have to be patient if you want to get there in the end but I was tired and my head rested against the wall and then slipped slowly down and it was only John's plastic bags that woke me up and he said at least I wasn't dead and he went off to his room and I got up and went to my bed.

In the morning Anna didn't look so good and the happiness that had been in her eyes wasn't there anymore and so I asked her if she wanted three sugars in her coffee because that always makes me feel better at the beginning of the day but she said no could she just have it black and so I had to make her another one be-cause I'd already put the milk in but I didn't mind I just wanted her to be happy again. She just sat there and I just sat there.

'I like the garden,' she said as she looked out the kitchen window.

'It's the best thing,' I said.

She said nothing and sipped her coffee a couple of times but she had to be careful because it was still very hot and she kept looking out at the garden and then she looked back at me across the table.

'Why is it the best?' she said.

'Because it's just something that's left on its own and it can grow how it wants and it doesn't have to worry.'

'About what?'

'Anything.'

I think Anna was going to ask me something else but then Jamie came into the room with his headphones on singing outloud some-thing about being the antichrist which was probably something to do with the Sex Pistols because that was all he ever listened to but I couldn't say for sure because my mum never had any records by the Sex Pistols she said the only punk band that ever mattered was the Clash and so that was all she ever played me and I remem-bered that when I read it in the paper that Joe Strummer had died I thought that my mum where ever she was would have been sad if she'd noticed.

Jamie nodded hello and started to make himself some toast while still singing that out of tune way everyone does when they've got headphones on and I could see that Anna wasn't going to talk about the garden anymore and so I asked her a question I'd never asked a girl or a woman before.

'Do you want to go for a walk?'

'Where to?' she said but didn't sound too surprised which was good.

'To the shops. We could buy cigarettes and then go and sit by the river.'

'Are you sure that's a good idea?'

I wasn't sure what she meant at first it sounded like a good idea to me and I couldn't see anything wrong with it and then she did smile and said sorry I shouldn't have said that and then I realised and I smiled as well because Anna could make even sad things sound funny.

When I went into the shop to buy the cigarettes Anna said she'd like to wait outside because the fresh air was nice and she wanted to make the most of it and so she did and I went in on my own and bought twenty cigarettes and two boxes of matches please because I'm always losing the matches and so why not stock up when you get the chance and I think the man in the shop thought I was simple or something but I didn't mind because it was a nice morning and I knew Anna was waiting for me outside.

When I walked out of the shop at first I couldn't see Anna anywhere and it was nearly like a bad dream or a film where everything suddenly goes wrong but then I heard knocking on a window next to me and I looked round and it was Anna inside the phone box smiling at me and talking to whoever and so I waited and it wasn't long and Anna opened the door and came over to me.

'I haven't been in a red phone box for ages,' she said. 'I'd forgotten what they're like.'

'Smelly usually,' I said.

'But don't you love them all the same, with all their little windows looking out at the world. I remember when I was a kid, I used to go and stand inside and count how tall I was by the windows.'

Anna looked very happy when she said that but then suddenly her face changed like she didn't want to remember anymore and so I didn't say anything about being kids or anything and when she said so where's the river then I just showed her the way and didn't even ask who she'd been talking to on the phone.

We sat at the top of some steps by the river that went right down to the water and I gave Anna a cigarette and lit it for her and then I lit one for myself and we watched the ducks swim over to us and hang around for a while waiting for us to take bits of bread out of plastic bags but then when we didn't they got bored and swam away because what was the point in people who weren't going to give you anything to eat.

'What is it with you and rivers?' Anna said as she watched the ducks drifting along to the other steps where some old lady was standing looking like her pockets would be full of bread.

'They give you space to think because you never get a river full of people do you?'

'No I suppose not.' She looked thoughtful like what I had said made sense to her as well but maybe she was already thinking about something else because her face had a faraway look and so I didn't say anything else because I didn't want to interrupt her and anyway I had my own thoughts to think about.

I wondered how long we could just sit there and not have to do everything else like having to go to work in the supermarket or listen to Zoë talking about star signs which was just something she did to stop herself thinking about her life properly. I looked into the river water that kept looking back at me asking me if I was going to jump in again only I don't think it realised that people drown and don't come back and that the tide takes you away before it's too late even to change your mind time and so really you've no chance at all. Except me and I'd had another chance but I didn't know why and I didn't know what to do with it but maybe Anna would tell me and still the river flowed and smiled by and that was okay by me I wasn't going to do anything silly this time the river could keep its secrets to itself I didn't need to be pulled into its world that went leading on forever to nowhere.

I closed my eyes and started to try not to think anymore and just to feel the world spinning slowly round but everything just goes still when you close your eyes and it's like the world has shut down and everyone's gone away and there's just noises of the ghosts of people and sounds that used to be alive and it's very peaceful but all the time you feel more and more alone like you're the one they left behind and you wonder if it's because nobody liked you or did they just forget about you because you weren't important enough and then suddenly I felt Anna's hand on my shoulder and I opened my eyes and the world was still there.

'I'm getting a bit cold,' she said. 'Is it alright if we go back to the house now?'

'Yeah, of course,' I said and I was going to say thank you for putting your hand on my shoulder but I've never said that to anyone not even Margaret although maybe I should have so I didn't.

When we walked back along the road I could see that Anna talked like me because she didn't say things unless they mattered which meant that we didn't say much a lot but that's how it should be for everybody if they stopped trying to fill all the quiet moments with words they hadn't thought about properly and that didn't really mean anything. That's what happens all the time and with every space filled then there's nowhere left to go. But with Anna it felt like we were starting to get that space back and maybe if we were careful and we didn't tell anyone else we could slowly build up lots of new spaces before people noticed and we'd hide some of them away so that even if they wanted to fill them all up again they'd never find them all.

When we got back to the house Anna said she was tired and needed to lie down for a bit and I said I had to go to work soon so I'd see her later but it would probably be quite late because I didn't finish work until 10pm. She didn't ask where I worked but I suppose it doesn't matter where you work or even if you don't it just matters who you think you are.

I waited at the bus stop again where the leaves always blow but they were all gone and I think it was the sucker truck that had come and scooped them all up because there had been too many to just disappear but there were none left on the trees now and so it was going to be a long time before they were back again and that's always sad but there's nothing you can do about it.

Outside in the car park at the supermarket Mark was having a cigarette and he waved at me as I walked amongst the cars and the people pushing shopping trolleys with too much in them because you can never have enough can you and it was good that he was there because I always hated arriving at work on my own with people watching you waiting to tell you what to do before you've even started.

'Is Vincent on tonight?' I said.

'Yeah, and he's just told me to sweep up all the leaves in the car park.' Mark didn't sound too pleased and I could see his point and still I wondered why everyone always wants to get rid of all the leaves but I didn't think he'd want to talk about that so I just said yeah Vincent is the biggest wanker like we always do and he said I'll see you later like he meant it and so I felt good when I walked into the shop even though the first person I saw was Vincent.

Vincent put me on vegetables which is the worst place to be because things are always falling on the floor when you're trying to fill the trays up and then there's always someone asking you about a vegetable that you've never even heard of and where is it like you're ever going to know or care and so you have to ask someone else and then no sorry we haven't got any anyway and I think sometimes people make vegetables up just to make you feel stupid.

The shift wasn't so bad though because it must have been a Monday evening and everyone stays at home then and watches TV saving their shopping for another day but still looking forward to it because if everyone really hated shopping then why do they spend so much of their lives in supermarkets when they could all have home delivery. I spent too much of my life in a supermarket I knew that but I didn't have any choice or that's what I thought then anyway because sometimes it takes a very long time to understand what it is you're meant to do and sometimes even then you get it wrong. So things were quiet which was good but still not all good because Sonia was working with me and if she had a chance to talk then I knew she would. Sonia was probably sixteen but much older than me and she must have been wearing makeup since she was ten and never taking it off and still never getting any better at putting it on.

Sonia came over to me and helped me lift the potato bag and pour the potatoes into the tray which was nice but I knew it would never end there.

'Have you got a girlfriend yet?' she said as two potatoes bounced across the floor.

'Maybe,' I said which was the wrong thing to say because it only made her more interested.

'You have, haven't you.'

'Not really.'

'What does she look like then?'

'She's very beautiful,' I said but it wasn't enough.

'Where do you go?'

'Out.'

'Yeah but where? I've never seen you out anywhere.'

'We just go to different places, quiet ones.'

'Quiet ones? Like the park or something?'

'Yeah something like that.'

'I've never seen you in the park.'

When Sonia said that her eyes were big and open and blue with lots of black in her eye lashes and she did have a pretty face but it was an empty one and I didn't think I could tell her about the river and finding the right space for your thoughts because she would probably only think I was trying to be clever. But still I did like Sonia because even if she did talk too much and ask questions that I didn't want to answer at least she did talk to me and wasn't like some of the others that I heard laugh and call me psycho when they thought I couldn't hear but I could and there was nothing I could do about it because you can't exactly go I know you think I'm mad but I'm not really and expect people to believe you can you.

'We've only actually gone to the park once,' I said although it was the river. 'Which is probably why you haven't seen us. And it is quite big.'

'That's true,' she said. 'Maybe we could all meet up for a drink one night.'

I said yeah that would be a good idea and we should do it some-time but I didn't say what time because Anna wasn't really my girl-friend even if I wanted her to be and I'd just have to see how things worked out because it's never a good idea to push your luck too far. Impatience is what makes sinners of us all is what Margaret would have said and I thought that maybe now I was beginning to understand what she meant.

Vincent called Sonia off to work somewhere else because he didn't like to see people talking and looking happier than him which didn't take much and so when Sonia said sorry I better go I felt a bit bad about not wanting to talk to her at first because she was just trying to be nice like Sally or Dougie and probably the world would be a better place if there were more people like that and not the sad ones like don't call me doctor Jane and Vincent who spend all their lives pretending to be important because they don't know who they are and for them the world will always be a scary place but you'll never hear them say it.

I got back to the house and looked into the TV room but there was just John watching the snooker and I knew not to say anything to him because he was very serious about snooker but nothing else so it was his thing and you left him to it. I walked back towards the kitchen thinking that a cup of coffee would be nice but when I saw Zoë sitting at the table with her hair now dyed blacker than I thought you could ever do I decided to go straight upstairs to my room and just look out of the window for a while and maybe have a drink later when Zoë would be gone. The stairs creaked as I walked up and especially as I went past Anna's room and so this time I didn't stop and I went straight on up to my room at the top of the house.

My room was an attic room or it had been once and now it still had a sloping ceiling on one side but as well as the window up there now there was one at the side and I don't think you can call it an attic room with two windows and also a proper door and no ladder to climb up but I liked it because it was my room and my room was a place where nothing could touch me and I was just who I wanted to be and I could stare up at the sky like I used to in Margaret's house on the hill where the stars were always clear but the wind sounded like it was coming to get you and it would take the roof off if it had to but it never did and when it had gone away the stars would still be there only here in the hostel the stars were never as bright but still they shone.

I lay back on my bed and looked up at the night which was dark and probably without a moon and I could hear bursts of rain smattering over my window like someone was throwing tiny stones but I knew they weren't because I could see the beginnings of small trickles of water sliding down my window not sure how they got there or where they would be going. I tried not to think about anything only the rain and the darkness of the night but you can't do that for long because all the time all the other things are creeping up and you don't know which one's going to get you first so you have to be ready for them all and there's always more of them than there are of you and it feels like you're being ganged up on and there's no way out and no one to tell because no one will listen they'll just say you should stand up for yourself and pull yourself together or else they'll say they understand when they don't and all the time time is running out. I tried to stay calm like Margaret used to say and that the wind blows your worries away but it's not really like that is it and I started to remember my mother and when she used to take me to the park in the summer and I used to sit with her and watch all the other children playing and she'd say why don't you go and play with the other children but I wouldn't because my mum never took me to the park and so if she had then I wanted to stay with her and she'd say I was a stupid sod and laugh and sit and smoke cigarettes and I'd ask her to do smoke rings and at first she said no but then she did and when one of them floated over me she said it was my own little halo and I laughed but I didn't ask her what a halo was.

I sometimes don't like to remember good things like that because too many bad things can cancel them out and so they don't really count although still maybe somehow they do and it's something to build on at least but I just think it's too far away now and there's too much in between to ever go back there and so that's why I got up off the bed and went back downstairs to make a cup of coffee hoping that Zoë had gone back to her room to listen to loud music and dye her hair blacker again.

eight

The next daytime was not a good one it was the kind of day you
don't want to remember but at the same time you should because
there are always things to be learnt. Margaret used to say that all
the time and I thought that she'd seen so many days and all their
different things that she must have learnt a lot and it was all inside
her head but maybe that's something that made her sad in the
end because she didn't see so many things anymore only me and
her room and whatever they said on the radio and not the TV because she said that was for stupid people but it was okay for me to
watch as long as I didn't take it seriously. I didn't really understand
the not taking it seriously bit but I knew how the TV can take your
whole day away and you've done nothing and they've done it all
and then you do feel stupid and so when I went downstairs in the
morning the first thing I did was turn the TV off but maybe still it
was a day that I should have left it on.

There was no one in the TV room so I thought I'd sit down and
read something but with even the old paperback books gone there
was nothing there and I knew I had a book somewhere that Dougie

had given me but it was up in my room and I didn't really want to move so I didn't and I just sat there with nothing which was nice. I don't know how long I sat there but it felt like a long time and then suddenly it felt like I was nowhere and I started to worry about things without reason. I started to think about Anna in the phone box and smiling at me but never saying who it was she'd been talking to and I knew she could call anyone she liked and it wasn't my business but I never had anyone to call and so it felt funny and I knew I couldn't say anything but I wished she would. When I lived with Margaret we didn't have a phone because we didn't need one we just had our-selves and we were good at talking to each other and maybe I did have to call the doctor once or twice but when I did I'd go to the phone box down the road and always tell Margaret what I was go-ing to do and tell her afterwards what they said because if you love someone then nothing should ever be a secret even the smallest things that don't really matter. I thought that maybe Anna had a lot of secrets and that was okay but I hoped that one day she would tell me because I knew I would tell her everything and she was the only person after Margaret that made me feel like that.

I was going to have a cigarette but then I didn't because it al-ways makes you dizzy in the morning and it's not a good way to start a day because as well it's sad and lonely to have a cigarette on your own in an empty room when you want to talk to someone but there's no one there. So I got up and walked into the kitchen and started to make a cup of coffee to try and stop myself thinking about things too much. I could tell I needed to do something be-cause I kept thinking about secrets not being shared and how that makes you feel alone like I used to when my mother was never there and I didn't know where she was and I didn't know why and when you don't understand things because people don't tell you everything then you always feel worse.

After I stirred the sugar into my cup I stared down at the coffee swirling round and round with nowhere to go just waiting to be drunk and then that would be it and I thought about where the coffee had come from like Brazil or somewhere and how when it was growing it would never have known that it was going to end up in my cup and if it could have chosen would it have wanted to be somewhere else or maybe just to grow and die in Brazil and I didn't know how long John had been standing there and probably I looked a bit stupid looking for answers in my coffee but he didn't say anything he just said hello like he always did and so I said hello back and did he want a coffee or something but he didn't answer he just sat down at the table and looked out of the window and I thought maybe there was a tear in his eye and when it started to trickle slowly down the side of his face I don't think John noticed because he just kept looking out like there was something to see if only he could see it.

'Are you sure I can't get you anything?' I said.

'No thanks, I'm fine as I am.' John answered without looking but he didn't look fine.

'Would you like a cigarette?' I tried again.

'I don't smoke.'

'Sorry, I forgot.' And I don't know how I forgot with John not smoking always being such a big thing for him but I couldn't find any of the right words for him just sitting there.

'I don't want to be one of the dead people, I'm not ready.' He said it like it was going to be up to him and he would decide when was the right time and I could have left it at that and then the silence but I wanted to say something.

'Who is?' I said like of course no one is but then John looked straight back at me and I knew it was the wrong thing.

'It's something you should think about.'

'What is?'

'Dying. I know I'm not ready but only because I've been thinking about it. Death isn't something you can ignore, it doesn't just happen to other people and you have to know that.'

'I do.'

'Do you?' John answered like he didn't believe me and it wasn't a question.

'I've watched someone die,' I said. John was starting to annoy me like he knew everything and I didn't.

'That isn't the same.'

John looked back out of the window after he said that and I didn't bother anymore because he didn't want to listen to anyone else and there's no point talking to someone who isn't listening because it's like speaking without words so I just whispered to myself that I had to go to work now but still I hoped John would have a good day because he looked like he needed one. I think he heard the end bit because he said bye as I walked out of the door and I was glad he did that because there was something about John that I liked only he didn't know everything about death like he thought.

After I closed the front door I walked half way along the garden path and then stopped and looked up at Anna's window because it felt like she was looking down at me but she wasn't there and the curtains were closed and the house just looked big and old which was what the day felt like already so I went back to walking and walked out of the gate and across the road to the bus stop.

The bus came quickly which was good because I didn't feel like waiting for anything and I didn't mind when the old people pushed in in front of me because I could see that the bus was nearly empty but still I hope I've got better manners when I get old. I went upstairs and there was no one sitting at the back so I sat down there which is definitely the best place on a bus and I looked out of the window and I wondered if one day I'd stay on the bus long enough for it to take me back to Margaret's flat or maybe if I closed my eyes and like in one of those films that never make sense the bus would take me far across the sea to Connemara and drop me off outside the big house and Margaret would be waiting for me at the gate and she'd be standing up straight like she used to and maybe inside in the house my mum would be making the beds or listening to the radio and everything would look a bit fadey or fuzzy like memories always are and I could just walk right into it all and never have to come out again. I nearly fell asleep to try and make everything feel alright and when the bus went too fast round a corner I banged my head against the window and I looked up and out and I could see the supermarket so I quickly got up and went downstairs and got off the bus at the wrong stop but the walk back wasn't far and anyway I felt like walking.

I felt like walking away from everything from the stupid super-market and the hostel full of crazy people with Sally how much she cares and Dougie the man who writes psychiatric reports while he listens to U2 going on about it and why it's called the Josh Tree or something stupid and it's years old and anyway why should I care and then he'd remember and he'd start on the Clash because I told him about my mum and I wished I hadn't and I had to pre-tend to remember all their songs because he knew them as well but I didn't I only knew one and that was White Man in the Ham-mersmith Palais because that was the one I always wanted to lis-ten to but I couldn't tell him that when he was trying to be nice and not talk about U2 all the time.

Everything was going round in my mind and I could imagine John waking up one day and finding out he was dead but still not believing it and who would be the one to tell him and he'd only believe it when he was up there wherever with Norma and then he'd be happy again and the plastic bags would be gone and he'd probably never even bother to watch the snooker anymore. That would have been a happy ending but they're in short supply nowadays Margaret would have said and she would have been right and right then I realised that the only reason I was still hanging around was Anna and that was good but still it made me nervous if I thought about it too much.

I'd walked round the car park three times by the time I went in to work and I think some of the staff had noticed but they didn't say anything although Mark would have said something like what's up with you you twat but he wasn't there and so I just worked on my own and did what I was told and it felt like this must be what it feels like to be depressed and in a funny way I quite liked it thinking that I could have a condition and it would probably be best to be a manic depressive because that sounded like it could be a bit of a laugh but just to have something that was a name would be good enough but I suppose I was cheating because probably if you're depressed and you start enjoying it then you can't really be depressed anymore can you.

When I got back to the house it was dark but it wasn't late, probably about six or something, and when I looked up at Anna's room the light was on but her curtains were still open and I just stopped by the gate and looked. At first I couldn't see her only some old picture of Bob Dylan or Van Morrison on the wall because it had to be one of the two because she told me once in the hospital that they were the only ones worth listening to and I should try it sometime and I said I would and maybe one day I will but probably only if she plays me the records because I get bored listening to music on my own. As I stood there watching for Anna I started thinking how funny it is the way people say they really like some singer or something when they don't even know them and probably never will and they say listen to the lyrics like someone is talking to them but they're not because it's no conversation if you can't answer back and if all you can do is sing someone else's words then you should just keep quiet until you can think of some of your own but I wouldn't say that to Anna because I knew she was serious about her singers and so that was up to her I suppose.

I was going to give up and go inside because maybe Anna had just gone out and left her light on but then I could see her shadow moving up against the wall and then it was her and she sat down on a chair near the window and started to brush her hair. She was brushing slowly and moving her head to one side and then the other and I didn't know if it was the brushing that did that or was she listening to one of her singers and being with them and say-ing what they wanted her to say but whatever it was she looked calm and peaceful and I thought about that story where the girl or queen or princess or whatever puts her hair out of the window and the prince climbs up into her room and I always liked that story and I wondered that if Anna did that what would I do and would it really be for me or would she be hoping for someone else. Then Sally opened the front door.

'Are you alright Michael?' she said. 'You look like you're in a dream.'

I was going to say yes I am in a dream and why does that mean you might not be alright but I didn't because I thought that prob-ably Sally doesn't dream often enough to know.

'No, just thinking that's all,' I said and walked over to Sally and said thanks as she held the door open for me and I walked into the house. I walked straight into the TV room and watched what-ever it was that was on I don't remember now but I remember that Zoë was now painting her fingernails black and all she said was I'm watching that without even looking up. I didn't really mind I just wanted to sit and stare at something because right now there was too much going on in my head and I needed not to think about it.

When Anna came into the room her hair was shining like she had just washed it and put conditioner in as well and she had red lipstick but not too much and she was wearing a black rolled-up-to-your-neck jumper and blue jeans and I think some black boots and I noticed it all at once because all of it looked so good together and she smiled because I think she knew she was looking good and she sat down next to me.

'How was your day?' she said.

'Boring really.'

'That's a shame. Boring days are wasted days, you shouldn't let that happen too much.'

'Sometimes it just happens. Sometimes there's not a lot you can do about it.'

Anna smiled again when I said that and I could tell that already she was thinking of something.

'What about if you and I go out somewhere nice and have something to eat?'

I didn't expect her to say that and it was like she was asking me out or something and so for a minute I didn't know what to say.

'Well what do you think?' she continued.

'Yeah great,' I said when I got my thoughts back.

'Good.' Anna got up. 'I'll go and get my coat and I'll see you by the front door in a minute.'

By the time I said okay Anna had already left the room and Zoë said again without looking up so what's her star sign then you'll need to find out if you're compatible but I didn't even bother to

answer because if someone's going to talk to you while still looking at their nails then they don't mean it and they're just wasting
your time as well as their own. I quickly got up and went to the
toilet and looked at my face and my hair and they were both as
good as they were ever going to get and so I left it at that and
went out to wait for Anna in the hall. I didn't have to wait long for
Anna and when she was there she was wearing a long dark coat
and I opened the front door for her and together we walked out
into the night.

Walking along was good and we didn't say much because we
both knew we didn't have to and it felt like it was raining all around
us but not on us and when Anna held my hand I just wanted to
keep walking forever but then we got to a restaurant and Anna
said that was the one and so we went inside.

We sat at a table at the back in the corner and there was a can-
dle in the middle in a wine bottle with all wax down the sides. Anna
took her coat off and put it on the back of the chair and I did the
same.

'Do you like it?' she said.

'Yeah, it's very nice,' I said. 'I like Chinese food.'

'Good. I used to come here a lot a long time ago, this place must
have been here for years.'

'I've never noticed it before.'

'Really? I thought you used to live around here.'

'I did but I never went out much.'

'Oh.'

'I didn't need to. There was always Margaret.'

'Yeah, yeah of course.'

Then Anna didn't say anything and suddenly she looked down
at her menu like she was trying to hide in it and I was going to say
something but I didn't know what so I didn't. I looked down at

sweet and sour and chow mein and even pork balls that I don't like but then Anna said something again.

'Do you want to get the set meal for two or shall we just choose lots of different bits and pieces?'

'I don't mind,' I said and looked up from my menu to see Anna with her brown eyes smiling again and looking beautiful. I'd thought a lot about how Anna looked and how I liked her but it was only then looking up from the sweet and sours and with the candlelight bright shadows around her face that I realised that beautiful really was the right word. I think she could tell that I'd noticed something because she looked deeply into me and she felt very close inside me and then she smiled and said you choose first and so I did and we started with pancake rolls because that's my favourite and went on from there.

The food was good and we did more eating than talking which if you're in a restaurant is the right way round but you wouldn't know it from the two couples who came in and sat behind us laughing loudly and non-stop this and that and I don't know how they managed to fit in the eating and maybe they didn't eat much at all but I didn't know because I didn't want to look I just wanted to be there with Anna and not care about anyone else.

When the Chinese waiter who was about my age came and put the coffee down on the table he talked and smiled at Anna the most and maybe that was just because he could tell that she was the one who was going to be paying but I wasn't sure. When he went away we sipped at the coffee but it was too hot and we both put our cups back down onto the table and then Anna said it.

'So what was your mother's name?'

I didn't know what to say because I couldn't remember anyone ever asking me because why would they she was just my mum and not like Margaret who always wanted to be called by her name.

Anna opened her eyes wide like was I going to answer and was there anybody there or not and I said my mum's name for what felt like the first time ever.

'Roisin.'

'That's a nice name, it sounds like a waterfall.'

I'd never really thought about what it sounded like because it was just my mum's name.

'Roisin.' I said it again thinking about it this time and Anna was right there was a rushing about it and a sound of water in there somewhere but maybe it was more like a river than a waterfall but I didn't say that because I knew what Anna thought about me and rivers.

'Did you miss her when she went away?'

'I don't know, too much has gone on.' And I wondered why Anna wanted to know when really I didn't want to think about all that stuff.

'Is it hard to remember?'

'No, I just don't want to remember,' and I tasted some of my coffee that burnt my lips but I drank it down anyway.

'Why not?'

I liked Anna but I didn't like the way she kept asking when I didn't want to give the answers and I could have said just because I don't want to but I thought a bit more before I answered.

'Because she's gone and what's the point. Remembering things doesn't bring them back.'

Anna looked back at me like she was sad about something and I thought maybe she was sad for me but then she looked away back down at her coffee and I could see that she was sad about something about herself that maybe she was trying to talk through me.

'But anyway, I had Margaret. And she was always there,' I said to try and make things better for both of us.

Anna came back from her coffee and looked at me again. 'And even when Margaret died, your mother never came back?'

'No,' I said and looked away like that was how it was and there was nothing anyone could do about it and I think Anna understood and so we both took turns to take sips at our coffee because we didn't want to talk anymore about things that were difficult and that didn't have any answers in the end.

o o o

After the meal we didn't walk straight back we went the long way around the edge of the park because Anna said the street lights there were nice the way they looked like the old gas ones that I'd never heard of but they did look different and more interesting than the yellowy orange ones that just glow at you without giving out any warmth and for a minute we just stood there and looked up at them.

'It's like you could be in another time or a film or something,' she said. 'A time when things would go slowly and you could think about what really mattered. There must have been a time like that.'

'Yeah,' I said. 'There would have been. Maybe there still could be.'

'You think so?' Anna sounded surprised.

'Why not? Everything changes but sometimes the changing things can be good. Sometimes things get better.'

'Sometimes maybe, but not very often.'

It was sad the way Anna said that and then looked over at another street light like maybe it would tell her something she needed to know and so I looked with her hoping that it would. After that we walked back to the house and Anna put her arm round me and held on tightly all the way.

When we got in everyone was in bed or just in their rooms because the TV was off and everything was quiet and still and Anna asked me if I would show her to her room and I did and then she said she wanted to play me a record if I wanted to listen and I said I would and so I went in and sat on the bed as she took off her coat and started to look for the music she wanted to play. I didn't take my coat off because I wasn't sure and so I sat and waited and watched as Anna went through her pile of records until she found the one she wanted. She had an old mono small box kind of record player the kind of thing I'd seen in sixties films on the TV but never in real life and I wondered why Anna had one because she wasn't that old or maybe she was but anyway she must have heard my thoughts because she told me she bought it in a charity shop for a fiver and didn't it look good.

'It does,' I said but I didn't really care much about record players and I think it showed because Anna looked a bit disappointed before she spoke.

'It sounds great, honestly, just listen.'

And I did.

The songs were quite long and sort of quiet and sad and you could hear all the instruments and the singer had a loud voice and it wasn't anything I'd heard before and it was hard to know what to think about it. I listened to the words because there were a lot of them and Anna would sometimes sing some of them like the first song saying to be born again all the time but still she didn't say anything to me. It felt strange being in Anna's room and just listening to this music that wasn't like anything anyone would ever listen to but there was one song I really liked and it was singing about walking and talking in gardens that were all wet with rain and not getting old and that's something I still think about now and I wonder if the singer still remembers how he sang it and did he really mean it and does he still think it now because it sounded good then and sometimes you shouldn't forget and the guitars or whatever they were sounded clear like they were right there in the room with you and it all felt fresh and bright and when the next song ended I didn't want it to because now there were violins in there as well and I was walking into the music and I didn't want to come out again and I wanted to be lost with this strange music and somewhere in the middle find Anna and we could go anywhere then and not have to care about the world that always just gets in the way and stops you doing what you want to do and I tried to keep this thinking going but the record had ended and the magic was going away and I couldn't hang onto it and so I looked over at Anna and she was sitting still sitting on the floor and I thought that maybe I would have found her if I'd tried hard enough but now it was too late.

I felt tired and I lay back on Anna's bed and she looked over at me and I think maybe she knew that I'd been there with her only there just wasn't enough time because there never is and she just smiled which was enough and I put my head down on her pillow and I said sorry I felt very tired and maybe I should go and she said no I should rest on her bed and she would sit and play the music quietly and then maybe later sit in the big chair and I could stay as long as I wanted because sometimes you need to be somewhere else and I remembered Margaret said that to me not long before she died but she meant it as a good thing and so did Anna and so I closed my eyes and started to sleep with all the music still somewhere there inside me.

When I woke up there were lines of light coming into the room round the edges of the curtains and Anna's coat was lying on top of me keeping me warm. I sat up to try and see where Anna had gone because the room felt empty and I couldn't see her anywhere only a big red blanket curled up in the big chair and record sleeves scattered across the floor and one record still there on the turntable but not moving just sitting there waiting. I carefully moved Anna's coat to one side and went over to have a look at the record stepping in and out of the pictures on the floor and it said Van Morrison on it and Astral Weeks and I wondered if that was the record that Anna had played for me because she never said who it was or if she did I was too asleep to know. I turned and zig-zagged back through the record sleeves to get to the window and I opened the curtains and looked down at the bright autumn sun bouncing off the cars and wondered did it ever dazzle the birds or did birds just not notice and get on with what they do anyway and then behind me I heard the door open and I looked back and it was Anna with a tray with two cups and a plate with toast.

'Did you sleep well?' she said and put the tray carefully down on the bed.

'I did. Thanks,' I said.

'That's good.' And she passed me a cup of tea. 'Help yourself to toast.'

And I helped myself to a piece of toast and bit into it warm and buttery and I thought did Anna watch me asleep after she put her coat over me and did she smile down at me and not mind that I was in her bed listening to her music and I hoped that she slept well in the big chair and that the blanket was as soft and warm as her coat and maybe now if she was making me toast then that meant everything must be okay.

I finished my toast and drank my tea and Anna didn't eat any because she was humming a tune that I recognised from somewhere far away and I must have heard it in my sleep because all the notes were already in my head but I knew I hadn't put them there and it was good to hear them quietly outloud because

Anna's voice was soft and she knew I was listening but she didn't mind.

When I finished my tea I said I'd better go and Anna said I didn't have to but I thought I did because when things are good you shouldn't push for more just be thankful like Margaret said and your turn will come again. I didn't say all that I just remembered it in my head all I said was thank you and your coat is very warm and I hope you slept well on the chair. Anna said she often slept on the big chair I was welcome any time and it was nice to have someone to play music to. I said thanks again for the meal and the music and everything and I started to walk towards the door but then Anna came over and stood right next to me. She looked into my eyes and then gently she stroked my hair and kissed me once on the cheek.

'Look after yourself,' she said and I didn't know what she meant but suddenly I felt excited and sad and lonely and in love or something and there was nothing I could say so I half smiled and nodded and walked slowly away thinking I probably should have done something else but I couldn't.

nine

I didn't see Anna for a couple of days I think maybe when I was out at work she might have been in but whenever I was back she wasn't there and I knew she didn't have to be but still I missed her.

After three days or maybe four I saw her one morning at breakfast but she avoided my eyes and Anna had never done that before and I was going to say something to her but she looked sad and far away and so the coffee I was going to make I didn't. I went back to the TV room and I wondered if she'd follow me in and say just hello because that would have been good enough but she didn't and I didn't sit there and wait and watch the TV I just waited. I don't know why I couldn't just talk to her and say again that her coat was really warm that night and maybe we should listen to music again or sit by the river or even eat some Chinese food but suddenly Anna was different and I wasn't sure that I knew her anymore and I didn't know why.

I thought again about the phone box and who she was talking to because she never said and I always wondered and I thought maybe she'd called the number again and something was said that would make things different between me and her but I didn't know and not knowing is always the worst part. And I sat there on my own not knowing for probably an hour and then Anna came in and sat down next to me. At first nothing was said and the silence was like a beach empty in winter with only sand and sea and wind blowing with no voices only things that didn't make sense because they were too big and never ending and then Anna rolled two cigarettes in the brown liquorice paper I'd told her about and she gave me one but still didn't say anything. She lit my cigarette and then her own and I waited for something to happen and then it did.

'I'm going,' she said.

'Where?'

'Back to my life.'

'Oh,' I said. 'Where's that?'

Anna didn't answer at first she just smoked her cigarette like it was all she had left and when she blew the smoke out it was like a ring that could have been a halo but I didn't want to think about that again.

'My life is just something I have to go back to that's all.' She said it like it was obvious and sad at the same time. 'I've been away for a long time but now that they've found me there's nowhere left for me to go. It's time for me to go back. Maybe I always knew I would in the end.'

'Do you want to?'

'I just have to,' she said and I could tell that she meant it.

The room then started to close in around me and it was like Anna wasn't there anymore and a mist had come down and taken her away and that was it and there was nothing I could do but still I had to say something.

'Who's found you?'

'It doesn't matter,' she said. 'I have to go. You can't just disappear forever.' And she got up and just touched my arm gently saying she hoped I would find all the things I was looking for and then she was gone and I smoked my cigarette until it burnt my lips but I didn't care because there were tears in my eyes and I was alone without anyone and I wished at least Margaret was there but she wasn't and I stubbed the cigarette out and closed my eyes to the world because there was nothing left there that I wanted to see.

Later I went back up to my room lay down on my bed and waited for everything to end. It was about lunchtime when I woke up with the sound of a motor running outside my window and so I parted the curtains and looked down and saw Anna with a man carrying out bags to a van where there was someone else sitting in the front and I could see all the records in a box in the back and then I think Anna sensed I was watching and she looked up but I knelt down and I don't think she saw me and I just listened from then and a few minutes later I heard the van drive away and when I got up and looked out there was nothing to see and so I went back to my bed and tried to remember the songs that I'd heard that night in Anna's room but already they were all gone and probably they would never come back.

When we had the next kitchen table meeting and Sally said Anna had gone back to live with her husband and her teenage daughter and wasn't that good I didn't think anything was that good at all but I didn't say a word and I tried to smile for Anna and I knew there was nothing I could do and I just hoped that at least her life was going to be alright.

ten

I walked into work like I didn't want to walk anywhere and Mark came over to me as I was putting my jacket in the locker and tried to speak to me.

'What's wrong?'

'Too many things,' I said, 'all added up at once.'

He didn't know what to say to that so he put his hand on my back and said he'd see me later which didn't really mean anything at all and then he went off somewhere else and I walked straight into Vincent.

'Look where you're going.' He sounded annoyed but he was always annoyed with me.

'Sorry. Where do you want me to go today?'

Vincent smiled when I said that but nothing was funny, nothing at all.

'Don't tempt me,' he said like he thought he was clever. 'You can start on boxes.'

And so I went out the back to squash boxes and put them into a skip that would take them away to be turned into boxes again. It wasn't a bad job. Usually there was me and an old man with a shaky arm called Barry and we would do the boxes together and he'd talk to me about football like I cared but he did a lot and it gave him something to say and so I'd listen and agree that it's all about the money and it's not the same nowadays only this time Barry wasn't there it was just me so it was quiet.

At first I squashed some boxes and stamped hard down when they came bouncing back and I threw them in the skip like always but then suddenly I was tired and the job was stupid and I didn't want to do anything so I sat down on the step and looked at the boxes everywhere.

It was raining outside but there was a roof over the top of me so I was dry but still cold because the big shutter at the back was open and the wind was blowing over the rain puddles right into me. I was wearing my stores jacket but it was never enough to keep you warm when you stopped doing what you were meant to be doing and I think they probably make them like that on purpose to keep you working and not stopping to think why.

I was thinking a lot about Margaret gone forever and now Anna going off in the van and so why was I still here what was the point and I felt for my lighter in my pocket and I took it out and flicked the flame on and off and on and off but it didn't make any difference the flame was still small and I was still cold and so I stood and walked over to the skip and there was a newspaper near the top and I fired the lighter and let my hands shelter its flame from the wind and I lit the corner of the newspaper. At first it wouldn't light but then it did and when it started to crackle and curl it fell down into the middle of the skip and I watched as it scattered other little fires around it and I remembered again the faces of my friends when we used to run in the park and set fire to the bins and everyone would have said that this was the biggest bin ever and they would have all dared me to do it but hoped that I wouldn't because what if we get caught but I didn't care about that now only I wished they were with me and could see the cardboard boxes starting to crinkle and flash out small flames that were climbing up the sides of the skip trying to get out as slowly they were getting bigger and I watched as the smoke curled up under the roof and waited there looking down at the flames dancing and laughing and making a whirr of noise the way fire can when it makes its own wind that blows softly through it like there are ghosts walking in the flames and they've seen you but they'll pretend not to notice and you'll never see them until you're ready to go with them and I wondered if Margaret was in there somewhere and I tried to look deep and closely into the fire but it was getting too hot and someone grabbed me from behind and threw me to one side and then fire extinguishers were firing everywhere.

And I got up and walked out into what knows where and I could hear someone shouting that was probably Vincent and so I started to run like I'd never run before but I don't think they were even trying to catch me up and it was easy and I got to the bus stop and I nearly waited for the bus but instead I kept on going because I knew they'd be after me in the end and I didn't stop until I got in my door and I grabbed for my bag and I was still breathing like it was hard but really it wasn't because I knew what I had to do. I could hear John in his room with his plastic bags and still talking to Norma and where had she gone but I knew I had to go too because there was nothing left anymore and still there was something out there that I had to find and if you don't move fast soon it will be gone and I remembered

Margaret said that and right now as I squashed my clothes in the bag I knew without thinking what she meant.

eleven

I was walking again and I was cold and I tried to warm myself up with my coat doing up buttons and putting hands in my pockets but still I couldn't find enough and so I was glad when I reached the station.

I walked into the booking office and up to a skinny man with glasses too big for his nose that nearly covered his face and asked for a ticket to Ireland.

'Ireland's a big place,' he said.

'I know,' I said.

'What station to you want to travel to sir?'

'Connemara.'

The man did something on his computer and then looked up at me like here we go again.

'There isn't any station called Connemara.'

'There must be.'

'There isn't.'

'Oh.'

'I could sell you a ticket to Dublin or Dun Laoghaire.'

'I don't want to go to Dublin.'

And it came out stronger than I thought but I'd said it and that was that.

The man looked at me like what's wrong with you but I just looked straight back at him so he looked down at his computer and said that'd be Dun Laoghaire then sir but he didn't sound like he meant the sir bit. He gave me the tickets and said to get off the train and get the boat from Holyhead and I said thank you and paid with a bank card thinking that once I got to Ireland someone would know where Connemara was.

The train moved out of the city like it didn't want to go anywhere but after the stop starts it started to go fast and I was going somewhere and the trolley lady asked was there anything I wanted which was a stupid question but it wasn't her fault so I just said no and waited for the train to get to where it was going. And it seemed like it took forever and I watched the buildings turn into trees that just stood there in the rain not caring that time was passing them by because they'd seen it all before and it would all come again so why watch when nothing changes. And the fields were big and the sky fell down onto the hills that made you think that there was no room left to move but still the train kept going and I wondered where I would get off so I looked at my ticket and hoped that it was where I wanted to go.

When the train stopped outside it was dark and raining with bright lights to show you the way and as I walked on the platform I could smell the sea but not see it and there was a big boat with a hole ready for all the cars and lorries to pour in but I walked in upstairs and the ship was quite busy with people moving around looking for a seat for the night but I found myself one in the bar near a window that looked out onto nothing and I leaned back into the chair and lifted my legs up to rest on my bag on the floor and tried not to listen to the sounds of everyone around me.

I was drifting in sleep when I could feel the boat moving on waves being rocked and there was the murmur of the engine driving down below and around me I could hear the sound of Irish voices and it made me think of Margaret and the way she talked and until now I'd forgotten how she really sounded I'd only remembered the words but it's the way you say things as well and the sounds you make as you go along that are saying who you really are and maybe where you come from and my mum never really sounded very Irish she was London but that was probably only what she wanted.

I hadn't thought about it before but I was going back to a country that was in a way my own but who would think that and I'd just be another English one wanting to be Irish like all the Americans do and looking for ancient history but I wasn't I was just looking for a house to find something about someone who died in front of me and go back to somewhere where I could think all the thoughts I wanted and no one could stop me. I didn't want to be Irish or English or anything. Margaret always said keep your own history your own and don't let any country steal it because it's people that matter so I had to go back to where my history started to the things I remembered to when my world was my own and not what someone like don't call me doctor Jane said it should be.

And so I tried to keep clear about what I wanted to do but the voices around me were getting louder and some man was singing The Fields of Athenry that I knew but not enough of the words and he sounded like he wanted someone to join in and I opened my eyes to see him but everyone else was looking away because he was too drunk and old and even people who knew the words didn't want to sing along and so I just smiled at him once but I don't think he noticed because his eyes were watery with tears for things that he could never tell anyone about so I just got up slowly and picked up my bag and walked off to the way out to the deck.

I sat out there at the back looking down at the sea froth lit up behind by the ship's light that showed it all before it suddenly disappeared and the boat moved on with new froth and the wind was blowing across and getting colder and I hugged my bag to keep me warm thinking about how the wind was in Connemara blowing all over the house but never getting in and in the morning everything gone calm and mist hanging over the lough below and sometimes climbing up around the house so that even the sun couldn't look in but Margaret would make the fire to keep us warm and we'd eat bread and jam and drink hot milk with slippers on keeping our feet warm by the fireplace and mum was always tired and quiet in the morning saying just that it was good to be home when the world was far away.

I lay back on the bench and pulled my coat around me to look up at the stars and my bag was my pillow and I looked straight up into the sky but there were no stars only pieces of moon brightness that shone out from behind the backs of the night clouds that were trying to hide the moon away. But I knew it was there and it was telling me it was alright and anyway the clouds would never block out the light forever because morning would be starting soon and the brightness would push the night away and sometimes the moon would stay to see the day and you could see it up high faded in the background but still there just watching and the sun would never see the night and maybe that was sad or maybe it just didn't want to.

I closed my eyes then and tried to go to sleep but always there were the waves rocking the ship that kept waking me with a shake and three times I fell with one arm onto the floor and had to push myself up again and so I decided to just sit and I kept my eyes closed and rested but really I wasn't asleep and I was thinking back and I remembered there was one book my mum said I should read and not bother with the others and it was the one her dad sent to her on the first birthday she had after she'd run away to London and she was seventeen then and she didn't read it until four or five years later when he was dead and after I was born and she was alone. At first she read it for herself to think of her dad and how he'd never talk just smoke a pipe and read about the racing wishing he'd had at least one son and not just a girl that would never do what she was meant to do but still he had given her the book and it was a book that was about people's lives and love and a lot of it didn't make much sense but that's how it is and when I was older and would listen she told me about the book and read me her favourite bit which was right at the end. And I tried hard to remember and the book even had a name that didn't make any sense like it was Greek or something but the book was about people in Ireland and I could remember some of the words my mum read to me and it was something about a girl the flower of the mountain with a rose in her hair and *the sea the sea crimson sometimes like fire and the glorious sunsets and the figtrees in the Alameda gardens* and that was the bit I liked the best wherever it was meant to be and I always asked my mum if she would take me there and she said maybe one day we would go but we never did.

I think maybe then I did get some sleep without falling off the bench and all there was was the smell of sea air and the night and the chudder of the engine and me alone on the deck because it was cold and late and no-one wanted to go out there they were all wrapped up in warmchairs inside and sleeping or drinking and having the noises all around them that told them where they were and made them know that they weren't alone and everything was okay but that was for them and not for me I had too much to think and work out and so I needed to sleep alone with only the wide open space of the sea and the night time.

twelve

I was standing leaning on the rail looking out at the lights of Dun Laoghaire as the boat moved in over the dark water and now there were some people around me who wanted to see where it was they were going to and I thought that the lights looked quiet and sad like they were waiting for someone who would never come but still the people looked happy to be going there so maybe I was wrong or maybe people just don't see what they don't want to see.

When we got off the boat it was late and I knew that there would be no trains anywhere I wanted to go but I didn't mind because I didn't want to hurry and I didn't want to find where I wanted too fast because then it would be gone and so what do you do next and anyway I knew Margaret's house and Connemara would wait for me.

I walked along near the sea and it was a bit cold but not too bad and there was a sprinkle of rain but still not too much and I walked past the sea shelters where the old people would eat sandwiches and watch the waves and wonder if they would ever take the boat somewhere new watching as it crept out and went over the horizon but only now they'd be in their beds asleep and still dreaming of all the things you could do if you had the time or ever really wanted to and I wondered what it would be like if all the old people started to come out in the dark quiet night and sit down opening their sandwiches but this time with tins of beer and bottles of wine and talking and laughing and everyone else would think they shouldn't be there because there are things old people are not meant to do and when the policeman came along telling them to keep the noise down and haven't they got homes to go to they'd laugh and smile knowing it was good to break the rules if ever you can because that's the closest you ever get to being free.

And I walked on and then out along the harbour wall or pier or whatever it was called that was made of concrete and stones and stuck out into the bay and it went on like it didn't want to stop and then finally at the end there were two men night fishing and talking loud enough to scare the fish away and the smell of a night time's drinking blowing back down the pier towards me and I turned round and walked slowly back listening to the sea lapping at the sides of the cold stone like it was asking questions again and again but the wall wouldn't listen and in the end I knew the tide would take the sea away but still it would return asking the same questions day after day.

As I walked in away from the sea and past houses turning their lights off for the night I started to think about where I would sleep and should I try and find a hotel or something but I didn't want to start spending my money yet I didn't know how long I needed to make it last and anyway I was getting the train in the morning which wasn't that far away and the night was mild and so I thought I could find somewhere for myself if I just looked around a little. I went up and down another street with funny old Victorian houses and even one that looked a bit like a castle which in a way looked quite good but silly at the same time because when you think about it you should either build a real castle or just not bother at all and it was like that Englishman's house is his castle stuff that someone must have made up before they invented flats and bedsits. When I'd gone past the castle I went up another road that was steep with tall old houses with big steps up to the front door on one side and a park on the other and so I crossed the road to the park gates but they were locked and closed and everything inside was dark but still you could make out some red and yellow bits of metal in one corner and if you strained your eyes and looked hard you could see there was a climbing frame and a slide and maybe some swings but that bit was darker so you couldn't be sure and I rattled the gates but not too loud to see if they felt strong enough to climb over but they wobbled too much and so I walked away hoping no one had heard and looked for a way over the fence further along. I went nearly up to the far end of the street and still there was no way over and I was going to give up and not bother and maybe just go back down to one of the sea shelters when the fence stopped and there was a wall and where they were joined together there was a bit of metal sticking out which was just right for my foot so I threw my bag in over the wall and I climbed up and pulled myself to the top of the wall but having to be careful because there were some bits of glass sticking up but not too many so I stepped round them and jumped down into the park. And I fell onto soft grass that felt smooth and perfect as I rolled over like I always do when I jump down anywhere and I know you don't need to but it's something I started doing when I was small and by now it was too late to stop and why should I anyway and this time I didn't even want to get up I just lay there on my bed of grass looking up at the darkness and the sometimes pieces of moonlight that escaped from behind the clouds and I could smell the dampness all around me and it was fresh and clear and my coat was wet and it didn't care and then suddenly a shadow stood next to me and he was holding my bag and I sat up and he spoke.

'I'd get up if I was you.'

And I got up.

'I suppose this is your bag then?'

'It is, thanks.'

And I took the bag.

'You could have hurt yourself coming over that wall you know.'

'I was careful.'

'I could see that.' And he said nothing for a moment like he was waiting for the next thought to come along and then it did. 'So why would you want to come into the People's Park at this time of night, when the good people have all gone home?'

'I wanted to have a look.'

'You'd see a whole lot more in the daylight.'

'I've only got tonight.'

He looked at me like now he had something to worry about.

'You've only got tonight for what? For the rest of your life?'

'It's not like that.'

'You're sure?'

''Course I'm sure, honest.' I said it and I meant it.

'Good, because if you were thinking about ending it all the People's Park would not be the place.'

'I'm sure it wouldn't. But anyway I'm not.'

'I'm glad to hear it, there's too much of that goes on nowadays. The People's Park is for people not dead people, and that's why I'm here.'

'Yes,' I said because it was all I could think of even if it didn't make sense and I wondered if this old man was a friend of John's worrying on about the dead people and what happens.

'So why are you here?'

'I was looking for somewhere to sleep.' I looked at him and again he looked unsure and maybe worried so I said 'I've got to catch a train in the morning,' and then he looked happier but still not quite right and I could see that he had another thought that he was going to have to say something about.

'Why don't you want to sleep indoors on a bed? That's what most people do.'

'I haven't got much money and I wanted to save it for the journey.'

'Oh,' he said like I'd just reminded him of something important and now he had to think about that as well.

He looked like he was considering everything big that mattered in the world lost up in thoughts that were running into each other and he was trying to separate them out to try and make sense of them all but they were too many and there was only him standing there in an old battered green parka like the real ones they used to wear when they were riding their scooters but that was probably nothing to do with him he just needed the coat to keep warm even on a mild night like tonight when suddenly a boy has jumped over the wall and is now standing in front of you not making much sense.

'If it's just for the night I could show you where I sleep,' he said suddenly and I almost didn't hear him.

'Thanks.'

He nodded back at me like now the deal had been done and we were now on the level and he walked across the soft grass and I went after him and I could see ahead of us a hut or clubhouse or something but the wood looked old and bare and it was patched up in places and the kids had sprayed their dreams all over it and the broken windows were behind wire cages and I thought it was funny that the grass was so neat and tidy just in front of it but I suppose it would be hard to spray paint the grass or smash it or not bother to varnish it every year and if all you have to do is cut it and maybe just roll it every now and then you shouldn't really be surprised when it looks the best. When we got to the side of the hut the old man creaked open a big steel door and the light of a lamp shined out at us as he held onto the door and I don't know why but it made me think of a ship's cabin like a big old sailing ship from the Spanish Armada or something.

'That's to keep the vandals out and me safe inside,' he said and looked back at me explaining something I hadn't even asked.

And he held the door open for me as he showed me in and I remembered something and I was nearly scared but he was very old and now I was strong and so I walked straight in and sat down on the battered looking armchair that he pointed to and then I watched as he very carefully lowered himself into the other chair like he wasn't going to get up again for a long time.

'I'm the night watchman,' he said. 'They let me stay here to stop the place from being burnt down.'

'Don't you ever get frightened being on your own at night?'

'No. But sometimes very sad when there's kids outside with needles hanging in their arms, telling me to fuck off or they'll cut me, and there's nowhere I can go but back in here and there's nowhere they can go at all.'

'Will they be round tonight?'

'I don't think so, one of them died here at the weekend. I didn't like that, I didn't like that at all, it shouldn't happen.'

'I know.'

'That's why I had to ask you, I don't want anything like that happening here again.'

'No,' I said. 'No you don't.'

And then he went quiet staring away again and I thought maybe

I should let him rest but still there was something I knew I had to ask him and so I did that stupid half cough like people do which isn't worth the effort and why not just say what you're going to say without the silly noise at the beginning and use more words if you have to but we all get used to doing things for no reason and so anyway I did the cough and he didn't even move his eyes and so I just said what I meant to say.

'Do you know where County Connemara is?'

'There is no such county,' he said with his eyes now half closed.

I knew he was wrong but I didn't know how to say it because he sounded so sure and I didn't want to upset the man who'd just let me sit in his big chair and given me shelter for the night.

'But there is a place,' he said with his eyes now fully closed and sounding like he was going to go into some Irish fairy tale.

'Where is it then?'

'In the west.'

That didn't help me at all and I thought I'd just leave it and ask at the station in the morning but then the old man went on.

'To the west of County Galway from the lough out to the sea.'

'But it's not a county?'

'No and I don't suppose it's what you'd call a place either, it's an area, wild and green and nothing you can do with it.'

'You've been there?'

'I've passed through.'

'My grandmother used to live there.'

'Where exactly?'

'Near a big lough, I don't know where exactly, that's the problem and that's why I'm here.'

'You've come over to find a house that is somewhere in Connemara but you don't know where?'

'Yes.' And I knew it sounded stupid but what could I say.

'You could be looking for a long time.'

'I'm not in a hurry.'

'Good,' he said and laughed and then went quiet again and then added like he'd forgotten to say it in the first place, 'You'll have to take the train to Galway and then the bus up to somewhere near Lough Corrib. That's where you should start.' And then he looked like he was going to sleep so I didn't say anything only leant back on the side of the chair and tried to rest. And in the end I went to sleep feeling tired but glad that I was going somewhere and not just waiting for things to happen to me and for a moment I thought maybe that was how my mum had felt and that was why she left Ireland so that she could be in charge and do what she wanted to do which was good for her at first I suppose until she didn't know what she wanted to do anymore.

When I woke up my neck was stiff and as I straightened up in the chair I shivered and felt the cold in my bones and the lamp was still on sitting on a table a little bit behind me but it was getting light outside with sun starting to look in through the wire and the broken windows and I could see that I was sitting in the middle of a big room covered in dust with still some chairs stacked in the corner but nothing else really apart from a broken bit of blue curtain half hanging from one of the windows and the floor was wooden and once probably quite nice with those funny tile shapes and I wondered if the old people used to dance in here like the tea dances Margaret talked about although I never understood the tea bit. And then I noticed the old man's chair and it was empty and he was gone and I got up and walked over to the steel door suddenly thinking that he could have locked me in and I'd have to try and break out through the broken glass and wire mesh on the windows because you'd never get through a steel door and I put my fingers around the edges of the metal and I tried to pull and at first it wouldn't move and so I pulled a bit harder and then it started to slowly open and I blinked at the outside light as it hit my face and I stepped out into the People's Park or whatever he'd said it was and in the early morning daylight I could see the bobs of dew on the ends of the blades of grass and I always wondered how they managed to balance there like that and there was probably a reason and one day I would ask someone and maybe if the old man had been there I would have asked him but he wasn't anywhere and I'd told him I'd leave early in the morning and so I went back inside to the big chair and picked my bag up off the floor and when I went out again I carefully closed the steel door behind me and went off to climb out over the wall before any park keepers or anyone saw me and as I went I went past a bin which was full and I thought about how it would be good to burn like the ones when I was small and I even felt for my lighter in my pocket but then I thought about the old man and what he said about the park it was for people and not dead people and I let go of my lighter thinking he wouldn't want a fire because you never know what might happen and one thing always leads to another which Margaret used to say to my mum a lot and that there are consequences for all our actions and I didn't want any more consequences I had to find the station and catch the train so I just climbed up over the wall and walked off up the street leaving the People's Park behind me.

And I asked about Galway at the station and the smart dressed station man said I'd have to take the DART to Connolly then the bus to Heuston and then the Intercity to Galway and so I didn't understand anything apart from the Intercity bit and then when I asked he told me the DART was a train which still didn't make any sense but okay and that Connolly and Heuston were stations and did I want to know what a bus was as well and I said no and thanks and went quickly to look for the DART wondering if that was an

Irish word but probably it wouldn't be a good idea to ask anyone and definitely not the smartly dressed station man who I think didn't think from the look in his eyes that he was paid to deal with tossers like me.

And there was no train and so I waited and the cold morning air was fresh like it wanted to wake you up and tell you that you had to do something before you're dead and it could be long or it could be short you shouldn't hang around and so when the train came in I hurried straight on and found a place where no one was there and I sat down quickly rolling a cigarette and trying to blow smoke rings just to see if I could.

And I got the bus quickly from out of Dublin city centre thinking confused thoughts of my mum and not looking close into people's faces just in case and I was glad when I got to where my train was waiting once I could work out which platform and as it moved off I sat and tried to watch the outside and the town and then green fields but my eyes kept closing and I hoped that I would get there anyway wherever I was meant to go and there was rain starting to fall on the windows dripping down the glass and then blown all over by the wind and so in the end I watched the wet countryside fade away in the mist of it all as I fell slowly asleep.

The train stopped in some station that was all alone and no town to be seen anywhere and it stayed stopped waiting for nothing and some people sitting somewhere behind me wondered why until a railway man walked up and down the carriages saying he was sorry but there was a breakdown and we should get off here and wait but probably that was it until tomorrow now but not to worry there would be buses laid on and he didn't sound worried and his voice woke me up but that was okay because probably the air outside would do me good and already I'd dreamed that I was back at Margaret's house but got there too soon and I knew I didn't need to rush things so I got up and got my bag with all the people who'd heard it all before and would be driving their cars next time and the man didn't seem to mind he was only doing his job.

When I got off the train it wasn't raining and the sky was big and bright and the platform reached out towards nowhere which was where I wanted it to go so I followed it to the exit and walked through a car park that wasn't full of cars and looked for a bus stop that wasn't there and I asked an old man without a dog where do you get the bus from but he said if you don't want to walk then you'll never get to where you're going and he sounded funny like he was mad from being on his own too much talking to the shadows round the fire and never getting any answers but still like he said I started to walk because I didn't want to waste time just looking for buses.

There were stone walls everywhere like they were guarding the fields but who would want to steal them because they're there anyway and they just go on forever reaching up to the clouds although when you walk up close to them you can see that they never actually reach the sky which is in a way sad and so you hope that maybe one day they will.

When it started to get dark I was still walking and the town lights were nowhere and so probably I'd gone the wrong way but when you're searching for something and you don't know what it is I suppose there's no wrong or right way so I didn't mind really. I stopped by a big barn and looked into it to make sure nothing was there and it wasn't it was just hay or some sort of straw or something and it made me think about Christmas and Jesus and those stories they tell you at school even though everyone knows it's not true but still you go on about it every year and I always hated all that but suddenly I didn't and I thought maybe and I wanted to lie down and rest and I did and the hay was soft and it didn't mind that I was there and so I slept breathing in fields and farms and remembering Margaret before the Chinese takeaways and before she wasn't where she didn't want to be.

I woke up hearing the sound of a tractor like it wanted to get me and it knew I was in there somewhere so I grabbed my bag and ran again without looking back. I kept running on for as long as I could and it felt like I was getting somewhere and getting away from everything all at the same time and so I stretched my legs out carrying my bag like it was a rugby ball or something that I couldn't drop and I ran down all the lanes like nothing was ever going to stop me now only slowing down when my breath had started to run out and then I walked and walked and the sunlight started to come shining through over the going on forever fields and waking up the trees that were hiding in the corners and it washed my face and I smiled back at it all.

When I got into the town it was all still asleep but there was a man in the square trying to build something. I sat down on a wet bench and watched him and it was a market stall with a cover that he was trying to build but it kept falling down and I could see that you could never build something like that on your own so I slowly got up and went over to him.

'Do you want any help?' I said and he looked at me like he didn't but still he knew that he did and so I held a metal pole and he pulled up the other side and then there was a roof and he stood back and looked at it not sure if it was quite right but it was good enough.

'That should do it I suppose,' he said.

'What are you going to sell?' I said

'Shoes.'

He said it like that was it and there was nothing else to be added and so I didn't bother and I went back to my bench and he went back to getting things out of his van which were probably shoes but I didn't watch him anymore.

When I woke up I was cold and there was a fat lady sitting next to me eating chips which didn't make me hungry because I could see the dribble coming down over her chin and she was eating like there would never be any chips ever again. I sat up but still she didn't look at me probably because she was worried that I would ask her for a chip but if only she knew how much I wasn't going to do that but I did want to ask her something so I waited until she had finished up even the last broken one and then I spoke.

'Excuse me. How do you get to the sea from here?'

'Walk a bloody long way,' she said and laughed and so I laughed as well to be nice to her and then I asked something again.

'Which way should I go then?'

'Are you being serious?'

'I am.'

'You'll need to find the bus station first love.'

'Is it far?'

'Not as far as the sea,' she looked like she was going to laugh again but I think she saw the seriousness in my eyes and so she didn't. 'Don't mind me,' she said. 'You get the buses from the other side of the square round the back.'

'Thank you.'

'You'll need to get two though. The driver should tell you where to change if you tell him where exactly it is you want to get to.'

'I'm not sure yet,' I said, 'but I'll recognise the name.'

'I hope you do,' she said, 'or you'll be sitting on that bus an awful long time.'

I told her I'd remember in the end and thanks for her help and I thought she was quite nice really even if she did eat chips like it was about to be the end of the world.

When I got to the bus station there was no one there not even a bus and it didn't look like much of a station to me because there was no roof and just a little island in the middle of the road with a space each side for the bus to drive in or out depending on which way it wanted to go and right now no one was going anywhere so I sat on a dustbin. Nothing happened for a long time and then a man with a beard and no hair came up and stood next to me saying there should be one soon and I said I hoped so but he didn't say anything else until there was a sound of a bus coming with a chug round the corner and he said it was better late than never which Margaret said made no sense at all because sometimes late can mean too late and that's it and so you should do things now and not wait for never but you don't start explaining that to a man with a beard and no hair who wants to get on his bus you just keep your thoughts to yourself.

The bus drove into the rain like it was trying to find where it was coming from but you can never beat the rain it always gets there first and then it disappears and it's all over and you're just wet and there's nothing you can do about it. I'd told the driver the name of a place that was written on the side of the bus which was salt lake or hill or something saying it was sea and fun and maybe it was and maybe it was the right place and it sounded like somewhere I'd been but I didn't know because what I remembered about the big house was more about the sky than the sea because I was little when I was there and the sky is always bigger than the sea and I didn't remember any sand only green and the only water was the lough below hiding in the mist and I couldn't understand why I remembered these things and not others but maybe I would in the end.

The next bus was nicer, it was calmer and it didn't mind the rain and it was going to get to where it wanted to go anyway so why hurry which is the best way. And we passed through villages that no one would ever go to they just sit there on their own waiting for something to happen that never does and the people who live there don't ever leave they just die waiting. And we drove on with in between everything the countryside just out there laughing at it all until we got to the edge of the big town that swallowed up all the fields and so who was laughing now and it felt good to be back in the city because at least then you know what to expect.

thirteen

And as I walked down the steps I said thanks to the driver and he said take care now and I stepped out onto the pavement and the wind was blowing in all over the place and so I hurried across the street and went into the arcade with bright lights and slot machines and there was no one there only a woman in a glass cage in the middle who looked very sad. She looked young probably about my age but her eyes looked older and her mind was far away and she didn't see me and I didn't think she ever would so I walked over to a machine at the back and put my hand in my pocket to see if I had the right change. I took out a coin and that would give me four goes and so I put it in the machine and pressed the start and then the wheels went round until they stopped and there were dollar signs but no money and I pushed again three more times but the machine kept my money and wasn't going to give any-thing back which I suppose is its job but still it leaves you feeling bad. I remembered a big argument with my mum one day which might even have been here at the same place when she kept putting her money in and I'd said go on go on and she did but the machines wouldn't give her anything back and then she hit me when I got in the way and said it was all my fault and now she was going to stay there until she won something but she didn't look like she was going to win and so I said I think we should go and she hit me again and then she kicked one of the machines and the alarm went off and a big man came over and said to get out now but mum said no not until one of your bloody machines gives me back some of my money and then she started shaking the machine and the man got hold of her arm and pushed her out of the place and I was left in there with all the machines and the noise and I cried.

Suddenly I didn't know why I was in there and I didn't want to lose any more money or have to start thinking about my mother again and so I walked back out into the wind which is what it always is at the seaside and so what is a sea breeze anyway because it never felt like a breeze to me.

When I was outside I walked down to the sea and looked out over the concrete and then the sand to where somewhere out there the waves were crashing and falling down under the rain and I went on along the promenade holding my head right down against the wind but the rain was now slapping across my face so I turned back and went across the road and then in and out of side streets trying to hide from the rain that wouldn't leave me alone and then I saw a shop where the front was a bit sheltered with a sticking out roof and a bit at the side and I went over and looked in the window like I was interested. Inside there were rows of electric guitars standing up on their own and I started to read the names that were written at the top of them saying Gibson and Fender and then Stratocaster which I think should have said rollercoaster because that's what good music should sound like but I can't play the guitar so I suppose it doesn't matter. And behind the guitars there were amplifiers which said Vox which was probably a foreign word because it didn't make any sense to me and I thought about the records that Anna had played to me and I wondered if she knew what guitars they played as well as knowing all the words and did she ever see the amplifiers or did she just listen to the records and never go and see the people playing the music because she wanted to be on her own to listen because then the music's yours and you don't have to share it with anyone. Anna had shared the music with me though and I wondered why if she was going to go away and I was going to be left on my own not knowing what she meant.

I stood there and I could see my face reflected in the window and it was just me and the guitars and I was lonely and suddenly cold and I could feel the wind pushing in and waiting to get me so I turned around and walked straight into it waving my arms around and not caring who was watching because I wasn't going to let the wind win and I didn't care about the rain and the lines of water pouring all over me because I could walk where I wanted and nothing was going to stop me and I kept going like that all the way down the street until I saw a cafe with steamed up windows and a sign outside that said everything they cooked and it was a long list so I knew I'd like something because now the fat lady and her end of the world chips was a long time ago and I was hungry again and so I pushed into the door and walked inside.

Inside there were old people with old fashioned raincoats drinking tea and eating cakes and looking out of the window going it's a shame about the weather but do you like your bun and at least it's nice and warm in here and smiling and remembering when they came to the seaside when they were young and they could have been mods but maybe they were too old for that so probably it was rockers or greasers or teddy boys and remembering back then that they'd drink tea but smoke more cigarettes and maybe ride on a motorbike and dance and get drunk in the evening and back then there was no need for memories because when you're young everything is happening but it didn't feel like that for me and so maybe I was wrong about them but I didn't think so because they looked dreamy and happy and they were where they wanted to be and it didn't really matter what the weather did they just talked about it every now and then.

I went up to the man and asked him for tea and a toasted cheese sandwich and he told me to sit down and I did but not at a seat by the window that I wanted to be able to look at the rain falling everywhere but one at the side under a picture of a seaside town at night which could have been here or could have been there because you can never trust photographs and so I sat and ignored the picture and looked over at the girl sitting at the table by the window and she could have been looking out at the rain but instead she was stirring her spoon in her cup and watching the swirl of her tea and then opening the little packets of sugar and pouring them slowly in and I wondered if she'd ever actually drink the tea that must be more sugar than anything else. I kept watching just to see and I think it annoyed her because she looked over at me like what the hell did I want and I tried to smile and sort of say sorry but I just mumbled something that she didn't understand and she looked away again and went back to stirring her tea. I didn't look at her anymore because I know what it's like when someone is watching you and they won't leave you alone that's what is was like at the supermarket only they'd say things as well and laugh and it felt like they were trying to take my life away from me but still I knew all that was burnt out now and so it didn't matter and I would make sure that I didn't look at the girl again because she could do what she liked with her tea and it was nothing to do with me anyway.

After the man put my food on the table I looked at the cheese toastie trying to time best when to bite into it and I had a slurp of my tea but I couldn't wait any more so I picked the sandwich up and bit right in to the middle. At first it was good and warm and soft but then the cheese was burning and it stuck to the inside of my mouth and even if I could I couldn't swallow it because it was too hot and so I tried to spit it back out onto my plate but it wouldn't come away from the side of my mouth and so I had to stick my finger in and pull it out and the cheese fell like little bits of rubber onto my plate and I looked around to make sure no one was watching but the girl was and I could have run out of the place right then without caring about paying or anything only the girl smiled quietly at me and then went back to her stirring and so I kept myself calm and thought for a minute and then cut my cheese toastie up into small pieces so that it would cool down more quickly. I drank some more of my tea trying not to look in the direction of the girl again because now she had been nice but I didn't understand her and so I ate my sandwich slowly and it didn't burn me anymore and it tasted just warm and a bit salty and it was the best meal I'd had for a few days so I enjoyed making it last but when I was finished and I looked up again the girl wasn't there she was standing outside the steamy window and I could just see her and she waved at me and then she was gone.

I sat on my own then and wondered whether to ask for another cheese toastie but I didn't because the second one always makes you feel sick and I remembered that just in time so I went over to the man and paid him his money and walked back out into the wind with my collar turned up because that always makes you feel warmer even if you're not.

I walked back up and down streets that didn't know where they were going thinking that I was never going to get out of this town and I had to get back to the bus station and do what the old man said and find the way to Lough Corrib or whatever he called it because that must have been the one near the house and Margaret used to say lough and not lake and so it had to be right but still there was something about this town and I couldn't leave yet and so I walked myself back down to the sea where there was concrete all over the place and bits of rocks and I walked along the promenade and the sea was far away lost in the mist and sand that went on forever and I thought about how the tide takes things away and then some things come back again but not others and so do they just drift out in sea forever or do they find a better place.

I was feeling quite good and I knew Margaret would have liked to be walking with me but maybe she was out there somewhere watching me through the mist and she was okay now and I didn't need to worry and I said I wouldn't but still it was hard without her there because I didn't really know what to do anymore. I kept walking and when I got near the shelter a seagull nearly crashed into the side of my head and I waved out with my arm and told it to fuck off back to wherever seagulls come from and I hurried into the shelter and the girl was sitting there laughing.

'That was scary,' I said.

'And funny,' she said still laughing.

I sat down and didn't know what to say next and she stopped herself from laughing and continued.

'It was funny you know. Are you alright there?'

'I'm okay now.'

'That's good. They don't come in here.'

'Who?'

'The seagulls.'

'Oh,' I said and then thought. 'Why not?'

'I don't know.'

'They must be stupid then, staying out there when they could come in here out of the wind and the rain.'

'Maybe they are stupid, I don't know, you'd have to ask them.'

I thought she was probably joking when she said that because it didn't make much sense but she was right about them not coming in under the shelter because I could see them all flying and walking about out on the sand where the sea should have been.

'Do you like the seaside?' she said.

'Sometimes,' I said. 'I think I used to anyway.'

'Can't you remember?'

'Not really. There's a lot of things all mixed up, that's why I came here.'

'To be mixed up?'

'To work it out.'

She said oh and looked out into the floating mist like maybe there was an answer out there somewhere and I wondered if that's why she was here too looking for something only she didn't know what or where it could be found.

We sat there under the seaside shelter not talking for a long time but it didn't matter and she didn't even try to say something for no reason and it was nice to be with her and I hoped she wouldn't suddenly get up and walk away and she didn't and all the time the wind kept blowing around the shelter like it was trying to find us but we weren't stupid like the birds and we would never be found as long as we sat there still just watching things and waiting for the sea to come back.

I listened to the wind battering away at the side of the shelter and it was taking the rain with it and lashing it down across the roof and then suddenly a big blast of wind blew the rain into the sides of the shelter and the girl without thinking pushed herself right up next to me.

'Sorry,' she said. 'Do you mind?'

'No,' I said.

'It's just that I'm so cold, I don't want to be wet as well.'

I nodded and it was good to have her sitting up close to me because then the wind couldn't get between us and together we were like a wall and not just two broken bits.

'My name's Fiona,' she said and it was the first time I noticed her accent and I thought she sounded almost Scottish but I wasn't sure so I didn't mention it which was good because she said later she was from Belfast and that never goes down well does it and I didn't know what she meant by that only that it didn't bother me.

'I'm Michael,' I said.

'Hello then Michael.'

'Hello,' I said but it felt strange to say it because we'd already met.

The thing about saying hello when there's only two of you and you're still there together is that then you're meant to say other stuff but we didn't and I wondered if there were things Fiona wanted to say but like me she didn't know where to start or was I just imagining it all and she was just there because she thought I was sad and alone and maybe she wanted to help me only she didn't know how but I didn't think I looked like I needed any help and really I knew that I didn't but sometimes people like you don't have to call me doctor Jane still walk into your life and do things for you that they should try doing for themselves first but Fiona didn't look like one of them her face was open and her skin was pale like she had real thoughts of her own that I shouldn't guess about only wait until she was ready to tell me and maybe that's why we were both just sitting waiting for it all to happen.

The grey sky folded itself away and then there was no sunset only night and I was going to make Fiona a cigarette but everything was wet and soggy and cold and then she lit a match and slowly burned shadows on the shelter wall and I watched as they flickered and still she said nothing even when the match flame burnt up to her fingers and I blew it out before the wind could reach her hand because I wanted it to be me that stopped her fingers from burning and when I did she suddenly looked very lost and I wanted to ask her all the questions that people always ask me but I didn't and I put my arm round her and she let her head fall on my shoulder and I pulled her in closer and made the wind go away and when the rain started stopping we both fell asleep.

I dreamt things I thought I remembered or were trying to come back to me and I could see my mother telling me I was the best thing that ever happened to her but I was a baby and I was crying and I wanted to tell her that it was just the beginning but I couldn't talk and she wouldn't hear me anyway all lost in the happy thoughts that you have when you don't know what's going to happen and then I was in a room with a teacher and my mum was sitting down next to me and the teacher was talking about the last straw or something and this time they would not be having me back that I was lucky I didn't get any of the cleaning fluid in my eyes as well as all over the books in the library and how could a ten year old do such a thing and I didn't listen anymore and neither did my mum she just squeezed my hand softly and on the way home she bought her whisky and the coke for me and we watched TV until she fell asleep on the sofa and I got the blanket from her room and wrapped it round her and kissed her on her hair and then went to bed.

I heard a boat out there somewhere sound the blast of its horn and it echoed like it was lost through the mist and my eyes opened to see nothing only mist clouds swirling and Fiona was still asleep but with her head sunk down on my chest and she started to cough and I held her softly and combed back her hair from falling down all over her face but I could feel how cold she was and it made me scared so I tried to wake her by just gently lifting her head but she just mumbled something and shivered and sunk herself down into my chest again.

'Fiona,' I whispered it but still like I meant it. 'You're too cold. Can you hear me?' And she just murmured again. 'Please, try to sit up straight.' And I tried to straighten her up and she coughed again but I knew it would be best for her if she was sitting up properly and then I could see how she was.

'That's better.' I said and she was now sitting up but her eyes were still closed and she hugged herself tightly with her arms held around her like they would never want to let go. I shook her gently and spoke.

'You need to wake up, we can't stay here. It's too wet and cold and the mist's coming in. It's getting everywhere.'

'Where would you take me?' she said suddenly softly out of nowhere without even opening her eyes.

'I don't know.' I said and I was surprised and I hadn't worked it out and Fiona's voice was spoken like it came from far away and it held me because in that moment I thought I recognised it but I didn't know from where. 'We just can't stay here,' I said and I put my arm back around her and pulled her in close.

And I said you need to be warm and can I take you home and she said she was home and there's nowhere to go and she held onto me tight but I knew that I wasn't enough and so I counted the money in my pocket and then I got her up to walk but she was weak and she put her arm round my coat and I walked us out of the shelter and up to the street lights with the rain beating down and us splashing through puddles and all the time getting wet but I knew we had to find somewhere and so I rang on the bell and an old lady took ages to answer and she said what time do you call this and I said I didn't know but could we please have a room and she looked at us shivering and said if it's just for tonight and I said that it was and we had the money to pay and she said come inside but wipe your feet on the mat and we did and went in and she showed us to a room that looked like it had never been lived in and I laid Fiona down on the bed and I wrapped her in blankets and then I sat down in the chair by the window and fell asleep without turning off the light but when it came to the morning it didn't matter because the sun shined into the room anyway through the broken curtains and Fiona was still asleep when I woke up to the sound of seagulls but I didn't move because I knew she was dreaming and I hoped they were good dreams and I knew she wasn't cold anymore.

I carefully opened the curtains to look for the sea and this time it was out there and the mist was far up in the sky with the sun hitting the shelter that was alone looking out at where Fiona maybe wanted to be. I touched my hand on the glass on the window to make sure everything was real and it was cold but still warm with the sun and I wanted to walk out there and put my footprints in the sand but I didn't want Fiona to wake up with no one there so I sat back down and wrapped my arms around me and watched Fiona breathing when she was warm and full of sleep and I hoped that she'd want breakfast with me before the sea went out again.

Downstairs it was cold and the windows rattled with the rain and the old lady put plates of hot food on our table and we ate it all like it was the best meal in the world and we didn't start speaking until we'd finished all the toast and even wiped up the fried up bits of egg that hang on to the edges of the plate thinking that you'll never notice them but of course you do and that's why you save them till last.

'What do we do now?' Fiona said and I wasn't ready to answer so I still slurped my tea.

The question was too big and no one had ever asked me that before like I might know and help somebody else decide at the same time and so I looked down at my plate and then she put her hand across the table and I just reached over and held on to her fingers because there was nothing I could say that would even make sense.

We walked out of the door into sunshine that sparkled on the wetness of everything and we held hands but said nothing and I remembered how John with his plastic bags had held hands with Norma when they were watching the snooker and then when she'd gone he had to sit on his own and maybe that was what he was still doing now and I thought about Margaret saying you have to hold onto special things for as long as you can and when they slip through your fingers you should never look back and I knew John would know what she meant.

We walked back down to the seafront and there was a man on the beach throwing a stick for his dog probably because he couldn't think of anything better to do and the ice cream kiosk was closed covered in posters for a concert by Daniel O'Donnell or someone like that to keep all the old ladies alive but now they wouldn't be out walking because it was cold and early and the sun wasn't strong enough to warm it all up and everyone was already waiting for the summer again that always comes along too late and then Fiona stopped me and put her arms round my waist and we looked at each other and the seagulls kept shouting but I could still hear what she said.

'We can't keep walking forever.'

'I know,' I said.

'Maybe you should just go?'

'Where?'

'To wherever you have to go to.'

'I'm not sure where that is.'

She didn't want to hear or ask anymore and she just hugged me and I didn't know what it meant only I hoped it wasn't good-bye and so we held each other tightly and some boy cycled past laughing but I knew it didn't matter.

We sat on the beach stones that went down to the sand and looked out at the sea that was calmer now and you could see right out across the bay and watch the small boats already out there fishing and with the sun shining down and catching the tips of the waves it was like everything was alright now and we could have been there at the end of the film and the music would have played to make everyone go home happy thinking that sometimes in life things can work out but that wouldn't have been us because we hadn't even started to work things out and so we climbed back up the stones that we slipped on with the sun behind us and we looked for a bar that opened early and made one drink last for hours and then walked slowly back looking for the bus station still not saying much only watching the people around us gathering like clouds.

I stopped by the bank machine to get the end of my money and I said Fiona should have some and she said okay and she was going to sit down on the bench and wait for me and so I queued up behind the man in the suit who knew that getting money out was a very serious business and so he was going to concentrate seriously about it and check his balance and everything and he wouldn't be rushed just because there was a traffic jam of people starting to line up behind him. At last when he'd finished and tucked everything tidily back into his wallet and then put it back into his jacket and started to walk seriously away I stepped for-ward and I did my numbers and took out a hundred and it came out in twenties and I held it all in my hand as I turned round to walk back over to where Fiona was and I could see the bench but there was no one there and I looked out amongst the people with that feeling starting to come and I looked everywhere that I could see and the feeling was getting worse and I ran up and then down the street with tears and loneliness starting to come into my eyes because I knew she had gone and maybe she had somewhere better to go but I wished that she'd told me and in the end when I stopped and sat down on the wall I felt in my pocket for cigarette papers and there was an old envelope with writing on it and it said thank you and I hope things work out and I didn't read the name because I knew who it was from and I squashed it into a ball and threw it out to the wind and I watched it bounce down the pavement until I knew it was gone.

fourteen

I went into the phone box and I dialled the number and nothing happened and then I remembered and I dialled again with the code at the beginning for England and Sally answered and said how are you where are you we've all been so worried and I just said I was fine but I didn't have much change and she said she could call me back and I said there was no need I just wanted to know if my room was still there and she said of course it was and when was I coming back but I didn't say because I couldn't tell her that I just wanted someone to know that I was okay and I hoped it wouldn't be too long but there were things I needed to do and I couldn't keep on waiting forever so it had to be now and then the phone started to beep and Sally said take care sounding like she meant it and so I said that I would and then everything went dead and I put the receiver down slowly thinking I didn't know what to think next only that I could never go back to that room because it was too far away now and really I only phoned because I wanted to say goodbye.

As I walked out of the phone box a coach stopped next to me and the people in the windows looked happy like they didn't know why and I smiled and an old man smiled back at me with his face that had seen it all but still I wanted to know more and there were things that he knew that I'd never see but maybe I needed to hear and I wanted to explain it all to him but then some traffic lights changed and the cars just moved and the coach slipped away and I was never going to say what I wanted to say so I hugged myself into my coat and stood looking at windows of hotels that offered nothing and I was close to thinking I should give up on it all and maybe Margaret wouldn't mind but I knew she was watching and I wanted to be where she wanted to be and so I was lost but I had to keep looking. But I knew I wouldn't find anything here near the beach with the sea mist falling and my hair dripping and I didn't want to go near the shelter and find Fiona not there and I thought maybe I should head back to the bus station and ask about the buses and how to get to the lough and so I started to walk half closing my eyes to the mist as it blew into my face and all around me lit up by the lights that were starting to come on as the night clouds were bringing night back with them again.

I went under a bridge and stopped to listen to the cars shuddering over above me because something about the sound was like the buses coming out in the yard behind Margaret's flat and I always liked the sound and I wanted to wait longer and remember more but I was too cold and wet even under the shelter of the bridge and so I had to go and I did around another corner and up along another street and then suddenly I stopped in front of a bar that I knew I'd seen before. It was called Donnelly's or O'Donoghue's or something like one of those names that mixes in with all of the others but I recognised the big windows with different colours in the glass that were pictures like you get in church windows but this wasn't Jesus and his cross or god or all of the angels these were pictures of trains big old ones going through hills and over viaducts and standing in stations and waiting at level crossings and I knew about all of them because my mum used to talk about all of it when she had her drink and I had lemonade and crisps and she was waiting for someone but they hadn't turned up yet and sometimes they never did and that would be the best and everything all at once started coming back to me and I felt dizzy and excited and scared when I pushed open the door and walked into the bar.

Inside the air was hanging like it was never going to go anywhere and there were a couple of old men sitting drinking at a table and two fat blokes playing pool on a table under the low light that was built for gangsters but they had all gone now and it was just football shirts and pints of lager and I went up to the bar and waited for the barmaid to see me and it was long and she was old talking to a drunk man with a beard and laughing at everything he said and then she saw me and came over and though she was old she was nice and her dyed black hair might almost never have been grey and she smiled at me with red lipstick and only slightly yellow teeth and I asked for Guinness and waited too long like you have to but I didn't mind as she poured it like it was the last pint in the world and if she didn't get it right then everything would be wrong and when I sat down and stared into the glass I didn't know whether it was a shamrock or a heart she'd drawn into the top and I looked back at her to see but she was gone laughing with the man with the beard who would probably never be good to her but I kept my thoughts to myself as everything started to come back and I tried to make sense.

I sat down at a table right next to the glass trains in the window and I rolled a cigarette for later blowing the loose bits of tobacco onto the floor that still had old brown carpet that was never washed and the barmaid was still laughing and I could hear the clink crack of the pool balls and in the corner there was the juke box but the sound of no music and I wanted to remember things but there were too many signs. I sat back in my chair and smoked with closed eyes as everything around me still went on and I tried to go back to when I was there before but suddenly there was a sound right next to me and I quickly opened my eyes and the barmaid was standing in front of me.

'Are you alright there? I'm sorry if I woke you up,' she said and smiled as she picked up a dead glass from the edge of the table.

'It's okay,' I said and sat up more straight.

'Daydreams are the best ones,' she said.

'I'm just a bit tired.'

'Just up for the day then are you?'

'I think so.'

She looked back at me like why didn't I know but there was kindness in her eyes underneath the eye shadow and I knew she wouldn't ask she just wondered that's all.

'Yeah, for the day,' I said to make it sound better but really I didn't need to and she nodded like she knew what days could be like and said she'd leave me to my dreams then and went off looking for more glasses and so I didn't have the chance to explain that I wasn't dreaming that there were real things there at the back of my mind that I was trying to drag out into the open before they got buried too far down and I would never find them again.

But I watched her as she went and sometimes I heard something she said or a laugh and she moved gently like she was a singer moving between tables slim in her long dark skirt and maybe that's what she would have liked to have been and not gathering up glasses and talking to men getting drunk in a place where they never cleaned the carpet. And then a man from behind the bar out the back somewhere called out Barbara there's a phone call for you and she went over and he said don't be too long and she didn't bother to answer she went straight out the back and then I recognised the man's voice and I remembered her name and right then I knew I'd seen them before in this place with Barbara telling mum she'd had more than enough and still a man at the bar would always buy her one more and I wondered did Barbara remember me but not me now me as a little boy maybe nine years old who'd go and sit outside on my own at the table when my mum got too loud to talk to me anymore and sometimes I'd look in but I'd try to look away because she'd be laughing too much with her arm round a man who was squeezing her bum and I'd go off down the street to the chip shop with the money the man had given me and buy chips and two pickled onions and then just keep walking in circles past the noises of pubs and up and down the side streets with little warm houses with their windows open and TVs on and the smells of summer food in the air everywhere around and me with chips wanting my mum to take me home to Margaret but knowing that it would still be a long time and I'd walk slowly back to the bench outside the pub and now the curtains would be closed and I'd wait and sometimes fall asleep with my head in my hands and my mum would rub my hair and wake me smelling of cigarettes and whiskey and we'd go back in a cab and her clothes would look messy and we'd sit in the back and she'd put her arm round me this time and say that she loved me and I'd lean in against her and fall back asleep.

Suddenly as I sat there with the drawing on the top of my Guinness disappearing I was remembering it all and I was getting close to Margaret's house but still not close enough because I remembered the bar and sort of the streets but then it was hard because I only ever came here sometimes and it was nearly always dark even when we went out down from Margaret's house to the taxi and then be gone and get here somehow through all the dark and maybe a moon and past crackled trees and then the seaside night lights waiting there like they never went out just always shining because there was nothing else they could do. And now I could hear Barbara arguing quietly behind the bar with the man with a name I would never remember but he was probably her husband and anyway she'd had enough of him always telling her what to do and she could talk on the phone for as long as she wanted and he could change the beer himself for a change and then he said something that I couldn't hear but that she didn't like and she told him not to bloody bother coming back then and a door was slammed and he was gone and she stood there sadly as the man with a beard said if you ask me you're better off without him but Barbara hadn't asked him anything.

I looked away out the window through the trains and watched the lights from the traffic jam outside sparkle and flash into the glass and I could hear the engines outside but all the cars were blurred into the trains and I could have stood up to look through the clear glass above but then everything would have looked like it always does and Margaret said you should try to look at things differently whenever you can and why walk in a straight lines if the world is round so I stared back deep into the glass trains with the outside lights wanting me to see them and I wanted to be with them and I wanted to step into the lights and ride the trains to wherever they were going and it wouldn't matter how long it would take because maybe then I could forget about everything and stop trying to find things and looking for answers that didn't want to be found and maybe there was nothing there anyway and I was making it all up just telling myself stories to fill all the gaps that are always out there all over the place and so you have to put some-thing in those spaces before they get bigger and emptier and the wind blows right through them gathering up all the dust and then blowing it all up to knock you down when you realise you've nothing left to hold on to anymore and that's how I felt when I watched Margaret die and then when I thought maybe Anna would make things get better she only made it all worse but at least I realised that it was down to me I had to do something I couldn't just wait for someone to come along and explain it all. There were stories out there but they were real ones they were the ones that made up my life and I had to find and understand them all and that's a thing you can only ever do on your own.

I looked back away from the window picked up my glass walked past the fat men with pool cues smiled at Barbara who wasn't smiling back and went over to the jukebox looking to see if there was anything by the Clash and maybe even White Man in the Hammersmith Palais because my mum would have played it if it was there but it wasn't and probably never had been and there was nothing by the Clash and that was good because really I didn't want to hear a song and especially not that one and so I carried my now empty glass up to the bar and put it down on a mat and if Barbara had said thanks or even noticed me I would have asked her if she remembered those years ago when I was small but she was again laughing with the man with the beard as hard as she could and I knew she didn't want to remember anything.

fifteen

I walked out of the bar into suddenly still autumn air that just hung with the wind and the breeze and whatever else you call it all gone and I didn't know where to go next and wondered if that was how my mother would have felt when she was nearly the same age as me and ran away to the city because she'd told me the story but never how she felt when she must have walked out of Euston or King's Cross station as a punk wanting everything but not knowing where to start. I tried to imagine it for her making her closer to me at the same time and she'd shown me the pictures of her then with short dyed black spiky hair and a ghost white face with dark lipstick and black stuff around her eyes and funny ripped tights with a short skirt and a torn shirt and a tie under an old man's black jacket looking angry and sad at the same time and there was never anyone else in the picture and I wondered if that was because she only had one friend and they always held the camera and I did ask once but she said don't be stupid and then I said have you any pictures of the person who took all the photographs and she said no and I said was it a boy or a girl and she said it didn't matter and she couldn't remember everything could she and I didn't ask again but I wondered if the person with the camera was my dad I'd never seen because the photographs stopped when I was born.

Mum used to say about living in the squat when it was late and she talked and I wanted to go to bed because she didn't make sense a lot but I wanted to know and she said it was a big house like Margaret's and old as well but falling down and they had great parties with even a band playing in the basement once and they were going to change the world but not like hippies because punks knew what was going on and they were going to fight it and not just drop out whatever that was and I didn't really get it what mum said but she sounded like she meant it. Only it didn't work out and I think she loved me then but it wasn't enough and I just kept on wanting her but she wanted to be herself and though she said lots of bad things about me she never said I got in the way of all that but I knew that I did and maybe that's why she left me behind still looking for something or someone but always getting it wrong with the drink making everything always further away.

And now alone I wanted to see her and say that it all wasn't that bad and sometimes we were good really but I didn't think she'd believe it because maybe now it was all too long ago but still I could remember the pictures and I wanted to cry but I didn't know what for and I hoped that she missed me and I hoped that she was there somewhere with someone who cared for her because maybe then she could care for me again and if I stood outside King's Cross station she'd be waiting for me there but what I hoped for was all mixed up with the past with the good and the bad things and I didn't know what was true anymore. And the street was getting busy with night time drinking people and so I closed my eyes and tried to think harder about everything that never made sense about how everyone always goes away in the end without telling you where or warning you when and then leaving you to work it all out on your own and make sense of signs that are hardly there and still I wanted to open my eyes and stop all the thinking and I did but it wasn't enough the thoughts don't go away they just go round and round in your head and so I started to walk and tried to get faster moving like I was going somewhere to at least make everyone think that I wasn't lost and that I had a place to go to and that my head wasn't full of things that I didn't understand.

The thunder boomed out and there was lightning on the sea and when the rain started lashing down I kept on going only bending my head down to keep the rain out of my face but already I could feel it starting to come through my coat which was cold and dirty and now at least it was a long war coat that looked like it had been in a war.

I went on and on around a stupid seaside town that still I didn't really recognise but I felt like I should and I walked across in front of a cinema that looked dead but the people were still inside and then a police car drove past slowly looking for someone or something to do and I crossed the road again to keep away from it all but outside the kebab shop a girl was being sick on her boyfriend and so I went past quickly trying not to look and then there was a sign for taxis blinking out in front of me and I remembered something and suddenly started to feel scared but I didn't know why and it was like a shudder or something and maybe it was just the cold and I pulled up my collar more and hurried past looking hard down at the pavement and I went on some more but then I stopped and looked back at the sign flashing red and it looked back at me like it didn't care and then I remembered it all and I felt weak and leant back against a shop window and wanted to get out of the place.

I slipped down onto the ground which in there under the shop's shelter was dry with just small streams of rain at the edges and I pulled my knees up and put my arms round them and rested my head on my legs and held on tight pulling all of me together away from the rain and what I didn't want to remember and I didn't rock I just held still and thought about the stars out there through the window in the roof in Margaret's house and how it was safe there but nowhere else and I wanted everything to go away and me just to be with Margaret in the house on the hill and then it wouldn't matter what the world did and we could hide away forever and watch out for the ivy stuff changing colour and the leaves being blown from trees but left to swirl where they wanted to and no one would sweep them up or take them away and the clouds would bring the night in and then take it away again to leave mist and maybe sun but it didn't matter if it was all rain and wind that rattled around all over the house because there was time for everything and we could just talk and watch it all.

But whatever I tried to think with all the good things that were there somewhere in my mind everything still went back to the night I got the taxi on my own and I sat in the front seat and my mum kissed me goodnight through the window and then stood back to wave at me with a man from the bar holding on to her and her smiling with a smile that was going anywhere and I just looked back and then quickly away as the car drove off. The driver was nice and said did I want to hear some music and I said yeah and he put the radio on and it was playing weird stuff because it was late but that was what mum always listened to so I didn't mind and we drove on and the driver kept talking when he should have been listening to the music and he was young and probably quite good looking like you'd want a big brother to be if you had one and so I closed my eyes and started to go to sleep with the night all around outside and just some of the summer night air coming in through the window. And I dreamt about driving out into the sea and being carried by waves with the music still playing maybe even the Clash and I got to an island where I stopped the car because the driver was gone and I collected up all the bits of wood and put them inside and then found branches and covered everything up and flicked matches down into the petrol tank jumping back as the car set alight and then watching it blaze and then explode like fireworks with flames and smoke trails in the sky and pieces of metal falling down onto the sea causing ripples of waves that would then go still and everything would be quiet again only some branches burning softly to keep me warm through the night and then the next day early in the morning I would swim home.

Then suddenly I woke up and the car had stopped far away from the town in a car park with steps that went down to the sea and there was nothing else except a pile of building rubbish in the corner and I said why have we stopped here and the driver said he liked to look at the sea with the moon coming down and I should look too and it wouldn't take long and I didn't mind did I. And I said I didn't and he moved closer and said you can't be cold on a night like this and I said I wasn't and he put his hand on my leg and said then why are you shaking and I said I wasn't but this time I was and he started to stroke my leg and then put his other hand behind my neck and pulled me towards him and he turned my head and started licking my ear and I felt sick and I pushed him back and he grabbed my leg hard and said now be a good boy it's only a bit of fun you'll enjoy it if you give it a chance and he came for me again with his face smiling like he'd got me anyway and there was nothing I could do about it and I let him come closer and he said that's better with his face right up to mine and then I spat into his eyes with all the spit I had and he said you dirty fucking something and I grabbed for the door but it was locked and so I went to climb out of the open window and he grabbed my leg and it hurt and he pulled and I screamed the loudest I could and for a moment he let go and I fell down onto the ground smashing my face and I pulled myself up and I ran and I ran and I couldn't see or hear anything I just crashed out into the night along a road that was next to the sea but going into nowhere with no lights only the moon behind me and then the sound of a car and I looked over my shoulder and I couldn't be sure but I thought it was the taxi and so I ran off the road and jumped over a wall falling on sand and stones and I tried to keep running but now it was hard with the sand dragging me down and up on the road I could hear a car going slowly and I knew it was him and I had to find somewhere to hide and I looked and there was nowhere and so I ran some more until then the car stopped up on the road ahead of me and I stood still and I waited not wanting to breathe and then I saw him coming down the steps and I looked again for somewhere to hide and there was just one old small hut that looked like it was full of broken deck chairs and there was no window where the window should have been and so I climbed up and crawled in trying to slide under the deck chairs quietly to get to the back of the hut and sit crouched in the corner hoping for someone to save me that probably they never would.

I could hear the sea lapping up the beach slowly because the night was very still and so it was even harder for me to be quiet with everything else quiet already just waiting for me to make one sound and then he'd find me here on my own and do what he wanted to do and then put me in the sea for the tide to take me away and by then I wouldn't know or care because it would all be over and I wouldn't be me anymore I would be just nothing like all the dead people and I kept thinking on and on about being dead and reaching the end but I didn't want to get hurt I didn't want him to hurt me and I heard footsteps outside the hut and I stopped myself from breathing but then I couldn't anymore and I let out some air like a hiss and the footsteps stopped and then a head leaned in through the window hole and it was the man and I could see him through edges of deckchairs with the moonlight behind him over his shoulder but I kept like a statue but with a heart that was beating too loud but he didn't hear and his head went away and then footsteps walked off but still I didn't move I didn't know where he'd be waiting and I didn't sleep I just sat there all night listening and even when the sun started to creep into the hut in the morning and I could hear seagulls shouting I didn't go out in case he was waiting for the daylight to get me and then I heard some people walking past and then a dog barking and it wouldn't go away and it was barking at the hut and it knew I was there and I was starting to move when the door opened and an old man with a red face said who's there and I said me and I wanted to cry and he said what's the matter and what are you doing here but I couldn't say and I didn't know where to start and I think he could see the tears in my eyes and he said it's alright you can come out now and he held out his hand and I was scared but I took it and he got me to sit on the step at the front and he said are you cold and I quickly said no but he still gave me a rug which I put over my knees and he said your face looks like it's taken a battering and I'd forgotten about that and he said who should we call and I didn't know and an old lady came over and he called her my love and they talked and she said she would looking sad and smiling at me at the same time and the old man said off you go then and take care now young fella and I nodded and the old lady took me by the hand walking me slowly away as the sea washed up the shore with the wind.

And I was still sitting on the pavement and it was all coming back to me like those gates had opened up all at once all the scary and sad things you don't want to know about anymore because there's nothing you can do to change them so why think about them there are too many things out there to hurt you you should just try to think about the good things like I tried to tell Anna and how Margaret had told me but it's hard and sometimes you're not ready and then there's nothing you can do and something comes back you'd always wanted to forget and it wasn't as bad as it could have been but still it was the scariest night time of my life that I never talked about because no one would ever believe me because I was always running off and hiding in places that I shouldn't have been in and anyway I didn't want to upset Margaret or get her cross with my mum who still hit me for all the trouble even when the policeman had said a good talking to was what I needed but Margaret made me toast in the end and said to go to bed and when you wake up we can all start again.

I unlocked my hands from across my knees and pulled myself up wanting to walk into the rain and wash everything off me and the streets were still wet but the rain had gone and so I stood there looking not knowing where to go with the taxi sign blinking above and I couldn't think or even roll a cigarette so I just walked the fastest I could not wanting to see anyone or hear anything and as I went I didn't look at the railway bar with the trains stuck forever in the glass and I didn't look at my reflection in the big shops' windows or hear the two girls in little leather jackets call me a dirty blow-in I just kept thinking I was getting out and I had to get away and I walked on all round everywhere until I found the railway station and I went straight in and up to the woman in the ticket window and said I wanted to go.

'Anywhere in particular?' she said and I could tell she was sick of her job and so why didn't she just leave and forget about it all.

'Dublin,' I said quickly.

'Which station?' She was still trying to be difficult and I knew more than ever that I had to get out of this place.

'The one in the middle,' I said because I couldn't remember the name.

'Connolly then. Is that okay with you?'

'That's fine.'

'You'll have to change.'

'I don't mind.'

'Good.' She thought for a moment then looked me right in the eye. 'I don't suppose you'll be wanting a return.'

'No,' I said.

Then the woman got the ticket ready and she said I'd have to change at somewhere again I'd never heard of and probably for no reason at all and I said okay and paid her what she said. I walked off with the ticket and counted how much money was left and then sat on a seat on the platform and made a cigarette that didn't want to light because the papers were damp but in the end it did and I tried again to blow smoke rings like halos but it just made me cough and the three boys on the bench next along from me wearing just shirts and no jackets started to laugh so I didn't try anymore and just wished for the train.

And the train came in slowly like a coffin and very gradually stopped. The three boys watched me as I opened a door and got on and I don't think they liked me they just thought I was funny and maybe they were saying I was mental or something but I didn't care as long as the train would take me where I wanted to go and away from the place I never wanted to see.

The train started moving and I looked out of the window and watched all the lights go away and then out into the darkness that looked back at me with my own face and I tried to look through it but there was nothing to see and up ahead in the glass darkness I could see a young woman with a child asleep on her knee and she must have been in the carriage when I got on but I hadn't noticed her and now I looked at her alone in the night and she looked far away like she was thinking about what to do next and there was tiredness in the way she sat there holding onto her child but no one to hold her and I thought about me with my mum on the underground going to see her friends who then didn't want to know because she'd drink everything they had and then not want to go home saying it wasn't fair on me to be out so late and so they'd let us stay but mum wouldn't go to bed she'd keep talking on about how it was when they all lived in the squat near Hammersmith Broadway and they'd go and see bands nearly every night and did they remember that time at the Nashville or the Red Cow or somewhere else. But they never did remember her friends wanted different lives and they didn't care that mum once talked all night in a bar with Joe Strummer about how to change the world because now they liked the world as it was and you can't live in the past you have to make the most of what you've got now which Margaret would have said but not meant it their way.

I knew I was thinking about too many things but still I knew that I had to find my mum and why didn't she even come to the funeral and I needed her with me I couldn't just go chasing dead people on my own anymore I needed her to take me back to Connemara and show me the house where everything started and where she used to live and why she went away and the things about Margaret that she'd never told me and I needed to know and what was it like when her dad was alive and even what was his name because Margaret only ever called him your grandad and I was scared to go to the house on my own even if I could ever find it because maybe there were other things that I didn't know but wouldn't want to remember like the taxi driver and I didn't want things suddenly coming back to me when I was on my own and couldn't make sense of it all.

sixteen

It was still dark when I walked out of the station and into Dublin and it felt like I'd been on the last train going the wrong way because I could see people coming out of bars and getting cabs home or looking drunkenly for bus stops and I'd only just arrived and I hadn't even started yet but I knew that now I had to and I walked quickly with my coat all done up and my bag over my shoulder and the night air was cold in my lungs and so I didn't need a cigarette but I needed to find somewhere to sleep.

I walked across the town in between people walking together in groups laughing and I just kept going to keep warm because I didn't know where I was going to end up but still I stopped a few streets later by a big building in the middle of everything to look at the map on the wall and some girls bumped into me and one of them said sorry and smiled and then the other ones pulled her away laughing and I watched them go and maybe the girl would have looked back if the others had let her but anyway she didn't and so I looked back at the map that was in a big glass case and there were little models of buildings on it and if you pressed the button it was all lit up like it was Joseph and Mary and maybe him in the crib and I looked to see if it said anywhere I could go. I saw a model of a post office on it which I thought was funny because there must be loads of them in Dublin and then I noticed the one for the Guinness brewery which was a good idea and then some courts and a bridge and other stuff and then somewhere in the corner a little written sign for a youth hostel. When I pressed another button a red light started flashing to tell me where I was and so I looked at the roads and over the model buildings and worked out how I would walk there and remember the way because it didn't seem too far.

I went off in the direction I thought was right but then got to the river with the bridge far away and the street lights not properly working and there was no one around when I thought I heard footsteps and I was looking down at the water and what if someone pushed me in this time and it wasn't my fault or even my idea still people would think I'd jumped like before and the footsteps wouldn't matter and no one would know and I'd just get pulled out to the sea not thinking anything anymore. And I waited but nothing happened so I turned slowly around to look behind me and then breathed my breath out into the night air because there was no one there and no footsteps coming and so next I hurried towards the lights and the bridge because over there and down a road somewhere the other side was where the hostel was meant to be.

When I got to the door it would have been sometime after midnight because I'd seen it on a big clock somewhere on a church but there was still a light on inside and I rang the bell by the door which was all glass and modern and not how I thought a youth hostel would be and I watched as a man came out of a side room and walked slowly over to the door. He only opened it half way like there were secrets inside and he wanted them to stay there and not escape out into the night.

'Can I help you at all?' He said without sounding helpful at all.

'I need somewhere to stay.' And I looked at him like go on and be reasonable for a change.

'It's very late. We don't take people after nine.'

'Are you all full up then?'

'No, but that isn't the point. You have to book in by nine.'

'But I haven't anywhere to stay.'

'If I break the rules for one…'

'Please, just for tonight.'

'I really don't think I can.'

'Who's going to know? I'll be gone first thing in the morning.'

He looked at me carefully like maybe was I dangerous or not.

'It'll cost you twenty-five euro for the night,' he said when he'd made up his mind.

'I've got the money,' I said and showed him the money I had left which was enough but not a lot more and he opened the door fully and said as it's quiet and I said thanks and he took me over to the counter at reception and I had to sign something and put my name and address and I gave the old one where I lived with Margaret above the takeaway and then I paid him the money and he said I don't suppose you'll be needing a receipt now and then he showed me to a big room with bunk beds turning the light on which didn't matter because there was no one there.

'You're on your own tonight,' he said and I thought that was probably how he liked it and he said you could make tea in the kitchen through the door at the end and then he walked away.

I looked around the room and I could sleep on any bed I wanted but at first I couldn't choose so I walked slowly up the middle of the room and then back slowly again and I laughed because I felt stupid although no one was looking and then I stopped dropped my bag and closed my eyes spinning myself round in a circle for a couple of times and then standing still and opening my eyes looking at a bunk in the corner. I picked my bag up went over and climbed up onto the top bunk and sat with my legs dangling thinking I'd never been up on a bunk bed before and it felt good. Then I pulled my legs up and laid myself down with my bag beside me and I looked up into the cracks in the ceiling that the new paint couldn't cover up they were there and they would always be there and I liked that.

And I slowly started falling asleep with the light still on but it was better like that because I didn't want to be alone in the dark when I was thinking about all the things that had happened to me and the ones that would be next and I was nineteen but didn't know anyone now they were all gone and so somehow I would have to start everything all over again.

o o o

I walked out again into Dublin this time early in the morning before everyone was coming out to work and I went along Grafton or something street where a big tea shop was getting ready and I stopped and waited outside hungry for it to open because in the hostel in the kitchen there was only old milk and anyway I didn't want to wait I needed to get out and on with things.

When the door opened I was first inside and the place was big and old with high ceilings and like a museum only with a bit at the front selling bread and cakes and all sorts of other stuff like tea and even coffee and presents for your gran if you had one and then out the back where the roof got higher there were lots of little tables and people in waiters' uniforms and I went to the place where you queue up and got a tray although I knew I could only afford one thing because I'd checked the price and I didn't want to lose all of my money and it was a lot just for a cup of hot chocolate but I didn't want anything else anyway and as I stood thinking where do you stand to get the hot chocolate because there was no one else there and I was the first one so I had to work it out for myself I noticed a girl not much older than me standing at the side of the room and she was quite pretty with dark brown hair and pale skin and she looked over at me like where on earth did you come from but still I smiled back because I didn't care what I looked like and that my coat was tired and dirty I was happy to be there and I was going to order hot chocolate and then think again about what to do next.

I looked along and saw where the cups and the steam and the boiling sounds were coming from and so I walked up and said could I have one hot chocolate please to the man probably old enough to be my dad whoever he is and he just nodded and got the cup and did the pouring and mixing with milk and no cream thanks until it frothed up to the top of the cup brimming over the edges as he put it carefully down in front of me and said good luck and nodded again and I nodded back and thought did he always say that or was he just talking to me but anyway I moved along and paid the lady sitting at the till like it was the most important job in the world and you wouldn't get her pouring drinks for other people and then I went over to a table in the middle and sat down. I looked up at the ceiling far away up there and tried to imagine what it would be like just open to the sky and you could watch the clouds moving and bits of blue behind and the sun shining through whenever it wanted to and if the rain started to come the ceiling would slide back only this time made of glass and I remembered people said there was something bad about glass ceilings but that never made any sense to me because if you can look through to the sky and watch every kind of weather and be outside as well as inside that's got to be a good idea but then I could hear the Irish voices of people coming in for coffee to take out and my thoughts went away and I was back where I was and so I looked down and stirred my chocolate lifting the foam from the top with the tea-spoon and tasting the bubbles that were soft and warm and so I drank the whole cup with the teaspoon with the girl who didn't like me now laughing and telling stories behind the counter about what she did last night and wasn't she funny and great and her life was always fun and the man nodded and tried to smile and he probably didn't hear when I got up and said good luck because he looked like he needed it so I just nodded thank you towards him and he smiled back with the girl still talking and it made me feel good as I walked across the room and back outside into the mid-dle of people going to work with the background sound of cars and buses all wanting to go somewhere and get there first.

I walked on up through the shopping precinct and then crossed over a road to get to a park and I found a bench and just sat there trying to think and now starting to feel the cold again wondering if I shouted her name loud enough would my mum just come over and say hello and it's good to see you again but I didn't shout be-cause she was probably nowhere near and anyway she never got up this early in the morning.

I sat there on the bench getting colder and colder but there was nowhere I could go and I didn't know where to start and now there were people walking past me wanting to drop money in my bowl to make their days go better but I had nothing for them to put money in so they could save their coins and still feel good about their day while still I waited for where my day would lead.

I stood up and moved my arms to warm up and not freeze to the spot and I looked up and around and all the trees were there but sad as they lost their falling leaves that were brown and orange and stepped all over as everyone went to work just wanting not to be late but this time I didn't mind because I knew I had to move on as well and find a mother in a city I didn't know and I thought about all the mothers lost and there would always be too many to count them all but somehow I had to start somewhere.

I walked up and down streets full of cars stuck with engines on blowing out smoke that was wasted going nowhere and it was noisy like the middle of London only no Buckingham Palace or underground stations and probably if they were building Dublin again they'd put an underground in first but never bother with a king or queen because if you're not stuck with it you wouldn't want to make it up would you.

I don't think I walked a long way in a straight line I just walked in circles that gradually got bigger and bigger so that I could see things more than once and get to know the names but it had to be the English ones because I could never read the Irish words underneath although the way they were written and maybe sounded made me think of the sea and shooting stars and all the things you don't understand and I thought that if you had a book full of words like that it would look like it was full of magic spells and it must be good to know how to say Irish words and what they mean but maybe if you know it all there's nothing left to imagine and so in the end I didn't mind as I walked backwards and then forwards over O'Connell Bridge and then one time stopped and looked over into the river and wondered how many people had jumped into down below but knowing that I wouldn't join them pulled out to the waiting sea with everything taken away from them like they always thought they wanted and people behind glad or maybe crying and the bodies sometimes never found and maybe they're still living somewhere and no one will ever know.

In the afternoon I found a place to walk where the cars couldn't get in only the place was full of students and bars and I thought I could hear a band rehearsing somewhere but maybe it was just a radio on and the wind blowing the sound around and then two girls were speaking German or something in front of me and they looked back at me and then away and then they stopped and one of them spoke to me as I walked up. She was quite serious and I could tell that she meant it and she said did I know where Bono lived and I nearly laughed because it made me think of Dougie and he probably would know but I didn't so I said sorry no and she looked a little sad to hear it and then the other girl said are you a musician and I didn't want to say no twice so I just said yeah and she said do you play guitar and I said no to that and they looked a bit worried so then I said I played the drums and then they both smiled together saying they had a friend who was a drummer and so that made everything alright and they forgot all about Bono and they said things to each other in German and then what band did I play in and I made up a name and they said they'd heard of it but not very much and where could they get the CD and I didn't want it all to go too far so I said it wouldn't be out until after Christmas but that they should look out for it and they said they would and then I said I had to go and see you later knowing I probably never would.

I walked a bit more and then went into some film or art kind of place that had a cafe inside and I sat down in there to count my money which wasn't enough but like Margaret said it never is so why worry and I didn't I just counted and then went up to buy a coffee and a funny looking chocolate biscuit and no one looked at me like I shouldn't be there because I wasn't the only one with messy curly hair and some bloke even said without joking that he liked my coat and so I sat down again like maybe I was a drummer you never know. I looked over at one of the walls that was covered with posters for art things and gigs and plays and stuff and there was one in the middle I kept going back to and it was a picture of two women playing acoustic guitars who were going to be playing at some centre and they both looked a bit like they could have been in the Rolling Stones although not that old but with the long hair and bandannas like Keith Richards or maybe still they looked more like motorcycle girls especially with the one in an old biker jacket and that was the one I kept looking back at her face and it was hard to really see because the poster was black and white with the picture all grainy on purpose but the woman's face looked like my mum with longer hair and I remembered that she said she learnt to play the guitar when she was a punk in London but I never saw her play and anyway it couldn't really be her in the poster because when you go looking for your mum who ran away six years ago and only ever sent you record tokens on your birthday that you kept in a safe place but never spent you don't suddenly see her looking back at you in a poster telling you she's doing a gig that night at somewhere you've never heard of in a city you don't even know. It was a lot to take in and my coffee went cold as I sat thinking about if it was really my mum and should I go to the gig and if I wanted to I would have to ask someone maybe the bloke who liked my coat where the place was and so I did.

It was going to be a long time to wait for the gig that the bloke told me was only down the road and so I walked out along by the river right to where the big boats were filling themselves up with big metal boxes to take around the world. I sat down on my bag by the edge and wondered about what it was about this place that made my mum want to come here and leave me behind because it was just another city and aren't they all the same in the end only with the sounds of different voices and still it's always the place where you can lose yourself and I thought about when I walked out to the bridge when I had nowhere to go but this time walking I didn't feel the same something inside me was changing but I didn't know what. And I watched a boat move off and it was so slow and heavy it looked like it could never get anywhere but still it moved on and it would get there in the end and maybe that's what we all do without really knowing it.

When I got to the hall I was suddenly worried that you might have to pay and I wouldn't have enough so I'd have to sneak to get in but there was no one at the door and so I walked right in like I had a ticket in my pocket and so if anyone jumped up and to ask where was I going I was the man in the right place and they shouldn't ask any questions.

There were quite a lot of people in there already sitting or standing around some tables at the back and then up the front an open space in front of the small stage and most of the people were a lot older than me and looked like the kind who would go out at night and listen to acoustic guitars and it made me think of Anna and all her Bob Dylan and Van Morrison and I wouldn't have been surprised if she had turned up except that she disappeared somewhere in England and one coincidence if it really was my mum was probably going to be enough for one night. I rolled my cigarette standing in a corner at the back because I wanted to see everyone before they saw me especially my mum and I felt nervous and strange not knowing whether I wanted it to be her or not because what would I say if I said anything at all and would she want to see me or even recognise me if she did because I was a lot taller and older and my hair was long and I knew Margaret had never taken any pictures of me to send to her even if she had asked because she said if your mum wants to see what you look like she knows where you are.

They played lots of old music which someone said was good to hear for a change and when do you get the chance to go somewhere where you can listen to Janis Joplin whoever that is but I didn't really care I was waiting to see who was going to come on stage and I made my drink last sipping it slowly and making roll ups when I got bored and trying not to look alone but instead like I was waiting for someone who was always late and I was used to it so I didn't mind.

And then the lights went down and people clapped not madly but quite politely and the two women walked out with their guitars and stood at the front and one of them talked into the microphone and said it was good to be here tonight and she hoped everyone was going to enjoy the show and they were going to try out a couple of new songs but don't let that put you off and some people laughed so I suppose it didn't and then they started to play and it was the one who'd done the talking who did most of the singing and the other one at her side only did bits but more of the guitar playing and I watched her closely with her hair fallen down over her face and every now and then she would shake her head back to make it go away before it would fall down again and she looked a bit nervous and maybe shy and I couldn't stop watching her and everything she did because I knew it was my mum and I didn't hear the music it was like a film with the sound turned off and no one else was watching apart from me and even the other singer had gone and I watched the long hair that I'd never seen before and the face that I knew hidden beneath and she never looked at me or anything she just looked down at her guitar and if she had to sing she looked far up and away and still I couldn't hear the sound but I watched her lips move and saw how her eyes wanted to hide but still she was there caught in the light as I stood in the darkness knowing it was her.

And it all seemed to finish too quickly with loud claps at the end and the other woman said thank you for coming and I wondered if my mum would say that to me and then they went away and maybe they were gone forever and I couldn't move I didn't know what to do and the lights came back up and I thought everyone would leave but they didn't and there was time for more drinking and some more of the old music and I watched them all queue at the bar and rolled another cigarette wondering where in Ireland I'd be allowed to smoke it and then from the far side of the room first the singer and then my mum hiding in her shadow walked slowly over.

I watched the two of them go over to the bar and people were going up to them and saying how good they were and even better than last time and I think my mum smiled and I'd never seen her be good at anything apart from drinking and I felt proud but left out at the same time and I wanted to be part of it but couldn't work out where I'd fit in so I just watched everyone being happy and even my mum and I knew Margaret would have been surprised to see it and it was good but I wondered if my mum still listened to the Clash or was it all just old music now because when you get older things have to get calmer I suppose and I wondered about the house in Connemara and my mum getting so far away and now nearly back again and maybe she was looking for something as well and I knew I had to ask her all these things but I couldn't move I just watched and stayed in my own shadow until everyone finally started to go and my mum went to sit quietly alone at the edge of the stage thinking all kinds of thoughts to herself as the singer was laughing with the last people at the bar and then I suddenly moved walking in between tables and up to the stage and stopped just before her and put my bag at my feet and she looked round and didn't know what to say so I stepped a step further and started to speak.

'You were good,' I said.

'Thank you,' she said.

And then there was silence and she looked at me again.

'Michael?' she said like a question I couldn't answer with her blue eyes opening as she spoke and me forgetting my name and why I was there because I didn't know anymore and she should have known anyway.

'Michael,' she said. 'How did you find me?'

And I felt like I'd done something wrong because she'd run away and now I'd caught her but I didn't want her to feel trapped I just wanted her to hold me and talk about the big house and how dark it was with only the stars in the sky and the two of us away from everything and she didn't need another drink because the air was fresh and there was sea out there somewhere to take us away but instead she just looked and smiled very slowly like maybe if it's alright with you it's alright with me but I couldn't say those words and then she just said sorry and I didn't know where to go.

'I should have come back for you, I'm sorry,' she said. 'But I was scared.'

'Scared of what?' I said but then she just looked away and then back at me and she got up and she put her arms around me and I stood still and felt her warmth against me and it was like it used to be but so long ago and I thought about Margaret dying and I was the only one there and I was angry and there was so much I wanted to say but not here so I just held on and I knew there were tears in my eyes but there was nothing I could do and nowhere I could go.

She took me out of the place saying did I need somewhere to stay and I should stay with her for the night and I said that I would and I carried her guitar and we walked across Dublin with nearly nobody there and we didn't speak we walked into the wind along streets that were now cold until we reached an old house and she opened the door and I went in and sat down by the telly and she went to make tea saying how many sugars like she'd never asked and she'd never known.

The room was big but with floorboards and not much in and the settee that I sat on was old and you fell into it like the one in the hospital and when I thought that I nearly laughed because I wondered what don't call me doctor Jane would think about it all and then again John because I'd found the person who had disappeared and wasn't dead and I knew he'd like that but still think about Norma who was never coming back and he'd want me to make everything alright because of the already too many dead people in this world but I didn't know if I could as my mum came back with tea and gave me my cup and sat down herself with her face full of questions I didn't know how to ask.

'So you liked the gig,' she said.

'Yeah,' I said and then there was silence I didn't know how to cross.

And I sipped tea and she sipped tea and she looked up at me sometimes and sometimes I looked back but then we'd both look away because we didn't know where to start and I thought that maybe I should get up and leave and not stay in a room that I could feel was starting to fill with the shadows of ghosts and shapes of things that there was no point remembering and when I put down my cup I knew she was looking and I wondered if I started to move would she try to stop me from going until then suddenly she spoke.

'Why did you come to Ireland, Michael?'

'To find Margaret's house.' I sat back into the settee not able to move.

'So have you been there?'

'Not yet,' I said and then waited for what she might say next but she said nothing and so I said what I'd been thinking for a long time. 'You never came to the funeral.'

'I couldn't,' she said and then rummaged in her bag for cigarettes and the words sounded the same as when she said she was too scared to come back for me and they were just easy words that didn't explain anything and I wondered if she listened to them the way she said them and did she hear how empty and cold and going nowhere they were and did she even care because there was no sign I could see or understand and she was just there and she was my mother but so what if that was it.

She offered me a cigarette and I took it quickly like I was going to get what I could and for a moment she looked surprised but then she lit it and then her own and sat back down as smoke hung between us and the cigarette tasted funny because I'd been smoking roll ups for so long and I couldn't drag on it properly and I missed the taste of the liquorice paper but at least it was something to do to drag and puff out and we could both hide there sitting there making around us smoky clouds and thinking whatever we wanted but not saying it.

'Who was my dad?' I just said it without thinking.

'Have you a list of questions there?' she said sounding Irish like I hadn't noticed before.

'No, just some things I want to know.'

'Some things aren't worth knowing.'

'Margaret said that.'

'She was right.'

And I could tell that the talking could have stopped there and my mum would have finished her tea up and said goodnight and maybe kissed me quickly on my forehead saying the settee's very comfortable and there's a couple of blankets behind and she'd be gone upstairs and I'd be left wondering so I tried once again.

'I'd like to know who my dad was or is or at least something.'

'He's in the past, gone, forgotten.'

'I can't forget what I don't know.'

'Maybe that's good.'

'Why did you leave him?'

'I didn't.'

So why did you leave me I thought but didn't say and watched as she dragged on her cigarette and waited for her to say some more and watched as she stubbed her cigarette slowly out and still waited until she looked back at me and spoke.

'He just went away.'

'How old was I?'

'A baby.'

'Didn't he like me?'

'He liked himself.'

'Did he love you?'

'I don't know.' And then she looked sad and I was getting too close and I wanted to stop but I'd gone too far getting to somewhere she didn't want to go.

'He was the one who taught me how to play the guitar, that was good.' And she made it sound like she wanted to mean it.

I said nothing at first but then I had to know more. 'Did you love him?' I asked.

'Probably,' she said, 'I can't remember.'

And I could tell that she did but there was no point asking anymore because maybe you can know too much when it's too late and it won't make any difference and so some things aren't worth knowing but still they're out there somewhere and sometimes you can't help yourself from looking and so she went on.

'Sometimes I wonder if he still plays the songs we wrote together because sometimes I nearly do. But most times I just want to forget.'

And that was it and she got up like I knew she would but kissed me on the cheek and said about the settee and then went to the door.

'Did he look like me?' I said.

She stopped and looked back but like she was far away again.

'No,' she said and then walked off into the hall saying she'd see me in the morning.

seventeen

It was in the morning and I was still lying on the settee and the house was quiet and there was some sun coming in round the edges of the big dark red curtains that were made of velvet or something and looked like they were a hundred years old with the bits of dust all over them being lit by the lines of sunlight that were getting stronger and I would have gone over to them to let all the light in but the room was cold and I could see the puffs of my breath and so instead I stayed warm under my blankets and I wondered about who else might live in the house or had slept on this settee and I hoped not that old wanker Spez that mum had run off with and it was probably him that had played her all the old records because he'd know who Janis Joplin was and when it was great to go to festivals and they were all free and all that bollocks but still I hadn't seen him at the gig so maybe he was just something else gone forgotten like everything else.

Then there was a knock on the door and I sat up with the blanket over my knees.

'Yeah?' I said and the door opened and my mum came in carrying a tray with tea and the funny looking Irish bread always looking like it was squashed that Margaret used to make with jam on it and she said she just wanted to make me breakfast because I must be hungry and she should have offered me something last night only she forgot.

'Thanks,' I said.

She smiled but shivered as she went over to the window to open the curtains.

'I didn't realise it got so cold in here. Are you warm enough now?'

'I'm fine,' I said because it was still a lot warmer than the other places I'd been but I didn't want to go into all of that.

'Good,' she said as she looked out of the window at her front garden with a small tree in the middle and I looked as well but then across the road through the big trees growing out of the pavement that I could never understand how that happened and over at the other houses the other side and their bricks looked dusty red and you couldn't tell that in the dark but now in the sunlight they looked proud of themselves and old like they'd always be there even with the people inside coming and then going and the road was quiet and maybe it was Sunday but I can't remember now and my mum just kept looking out like she was waiting for someone to come and I thought maybe she didn't want me to stay too long and she was feeding me up so I would go away and there'd be no point asking her about Margaret's house because she wouldn't take me and wouldn't say where it was anyway and so I just started eating the bread and the jam because at least I had that and then she turned round.

'Have you read the book?' She said it seriously and I thought what book and I hoped she wasn't going to go all religious on me because I'd had enough of that at school and the priest telling her he hadn't seen me for months when I told her that was where I went every Sunday morning not out to the park puffing on cigarettes and starting fires even with the wet leaves on top of the paper stuff in the bins sending smoke all over the place and why did she care anyway she hated all that going to church and praising the Lord you could never see who never made any difference to the real world anyway and the congregation people in their tidy clothes always looking sideways from their eyes to see what you put in at the collection and the clever ones already there with their envelopes with a smile or a nod to the collection man as they put it on the plate and no one would ever know but still I thought maybe now things for my mum had changed as she looked at me openly like there had to be an answer in there somewhere and so I waited for my best answer to come and then it did.

'No,' I said because I hadn't read any book and so it was true.

'Do you know the one I mean?' she said.

'No.'

'The one we used to read?'

She said it and then I remembered.

'The Greek one?'

'Yes,' she smiled. 'It's about a journey through this city.'

'Is it?' I said because I didn't know what it was about only something to do with Ireland and love and I found some rude bits in it once that I didn't understand.

'That's why I had to come back.'

'Because of a book?'

'My father, your grandad, always wanted me to come back to Ireland, that's why he sent me the book, to remind me. You have to have somewhere to go back to in the end.' And she had the look in her eyes like this was serious and she really meant it and now for her everything made sense and she looked pleased to have worked it all out and be back in the right place and when people have got like that they don't want any more questions like when you've built your house you don't move the front door and I always thought why not but it's something Margaret said and now for mum it was probably right.

'Dublin is where I'm meant to be,' she said and so I didn't ask about Connemara and the house on the hill and I drank up the tea and ate up all the bread as she stared back out of the window looking calm and sure but still somewhere else and alone with herself.

With the sun shining clear and cold and an autumn wind blowing across the street she walked beside me with her head up high like she was trying to breathe everything in all at once so that no one else would have the chance to take it away from her and she said she was going to show me the city and walking was the only way to do it and I didn't tell her I knew all about walking and felt like I'd been all over the place already and she put some money in my hand and said it was to buy a new coat and we'd find a good one together and though I still liked the old one I said thank you and smiled because I could see it was a good thing she wanted to do.

As we went I thought again about the questions I still had and would I tell her that I'd been back to Salthill and the bar there and the beach and the concrete and that I'd remembered the things that she wouldn't want to know and that I'd had to do it all on my own and nobody had given me a book or even taught me how to play guitar and now as we walked she looked happy but still maybe near that edge that's always there and did I want to be the one to push her over and so I just said I liked her house and had she lived there long and she said about a year and the rent was high but she and Clare thought it was worth it and I said was Clare the singer and she said no but Clare ran the Arts centre where they'd played and she was a special person that made you feel warm and alive and then she went on some more about how great she was and caring and everything else and it sounded like she was talking about what you'd want a mother to be and I suppose that was lucky for her and I don't think she realised about me as she went on and though even she put her arm round me she was still far away and not really talking to me just saying things to herself like a long list of how everything was okay now and that was how it would always be and she didn't need to go back anymore it was all about moving on and being true to yourself however you do that but still I listened hoping for her to ask me a question like how was I and what have I been doing or saying it must have been hard for you when Margaret died and I'm sorry I couldn't be there for you or anything about me at all but she was lost in herself like maybe she always was but not now because of the whisky and all the stuff she smoked but because something in her head had changed like she'd switched channels to the one that played the stories with the happy endings all the time and so she'd hidden the remote control and as long as nobody found it everything could stay the same and everything would be alright and as she talked I hoped for her that was how it would work out but when we stopped by a bridge that was only big enough to walk on and she said that this was one of her favourite spots and she could look down at the water for hours I thought just once about telling her about when I looked down at the water on the bridge like the Golden Gate and how I'd gone right down into the water wanting the tide to take me away and how it nearly did and then instead it sent me everywhere else and that's why I'm here now and I've got my story to tell as well and I looked away from the water and I looked at the side of my mother's face that was older but still pretty and some bits of her hair were blowing down over her eyes but she didn't mind or even notice and she was still like in a dream and then she reached out her arm and her hand held my hand squeezing it gently but still unsure and she said you've always been with me you always will whatever and I could feel the tears coming to my eyes and there were no words I could think to come from my mouth.

And after that she walked me round everywhere and I went with her because I had nowhere else to go and now Connemara was so far away with the house I could never find and so we sat in Stephen's Green and I said yes it was nice but thinking it was just a park and not like the People's Park with the night watchman and the wind from the sea and we went to the tea place and that was nice as well with the same girl who didn't like me this time serving the drinks and not liking me even more and no wonder I was with some old hippy woman and I quite liked that but still it was getting me nowhere and then she took me to her favourite bookshop which was funny because they all sell books and so what and do people have favourite petrol stations as well because they all sell petrol but maybe they do just I've never noticed and she said she was going to get me the book so I said I'd stay outside and just watch the people going by and she said fine she'd be back in a minute and okay I nodded and she went inside until I couldn't see her and I looked once more and she was gone and I quickly turned and walked away because I knew she didn't need me around she was showing me the sights that I'd seen before and anyway it was her book not mine and one day when I needed to I'd find books of my own.

And I counted the money she'd given me for the coat and it looked like enough and I kept walking on towards the station and it was the DART again out to Dun Laoghaire and I sat down letting the train rattle everything around in my head like lottery numbers that were trapped inside forever so you'd never win but still maybe somewhere there was a chance but not if you kept looking for love that wasn't there anymore or remembering dead people that would never come back and John was right there are too many of them and if you don't believe in ghosts or god you have to find something else and maybe I would talk to Dougie again and give him a chance because maybe U2 aren't really all that bad and there were other things he could say that I hadn't listened to before and I would go back to what I knew and try and sort it all out from there and I wasn't going to just hang around and wait for people to leave me anymore I was going to build my own life and invite in the people who mattered or cared about me and not always just be there on somebody else's doorstep and maybe I would listen to White Man in the Hammersmith Palais one more time but then that would be it.

I got off the train and walked down by the People's Park looking in towards the hut thinking that probably the night watchman wouldn't be there now because it would be a long time until it was dark but where did he go during the day and I looked as I walked on down the street to the sea in case he might be around somewhere but probably he didn't like to be seen and maybe he was watching me and everybody else but you wouldn't catch sight of him and I thought maybe that's how I should be at the edge of everything and only making contact when you wanted to and so you couldn't be taken in by anyone you'd watch until you'd seen enough to know what they were really like and then you'd know what to do and you could hit and then run and disappear into the high hills like Bonnie and Clyde or especially Butch Cassidy and the Sundance Kid and maybe that's why they always let us watch those films in the hospital and I hadn't thought it until now but maybe it was telling us all something and giving us a way out and though there were always two of them maybe that didn't matter as long as you had something else in your mind like the house on the hill far away but always there and you didn't need to go and see it and spoil it all it was just there for you and you could hide out there whenever you had to and that's why I wouldn't get shot in the end because nobody would ever find me.

o o o

And I climbed up the steps and I stood at the top and as the boat moved out into the sea I looked back at Ireland and Connemara there somewhere in the rain and the mist now falling and it was good that it was there and Margaret would have said that and that was enough.